Z BOYS BOOK 1

An Australian Military Romance

SOFIA AVES

First Edition

Published by Little Quail Press

Cover Design by Kay Maszek

Editing by Partners in Crime Book Services

ISBN 978-1-922448-39-2

Z BOYS

Recommended reading order

A TABLE FOR TEN
KING
JOKER
HEARTS
ACE
MISTLETOE & MAYHEM
RUSKI

BLUE BLOODED BROTHERS SERIES

Recommended reading order
BREACH OF DUTY
novella prequel
COLLISION
POLITICS & PAPERWORK
novella
BLINDSIDED
MUGSHOTS & CANDY CANES
novella
SENTINEL
IMPACT
DARK REFLECTIONS
short story
RECKONING

COWBOYS & WESTERNS

<u>SNOW ON THE RANGE</u>
Red Hart Ranch book 1
SIREN ON THE RANGE
Red Hart Ranch book 2
SUNDOWN ON THE RANGE
Red Hart Ranch book 3

<u>RANGER'S WISH</u>
TeXan Devils book 1
<u>RANGER BEDEVILLED</u>
TeXan Devils book 2

PARANORMAL ROMANCE

<u>TRICKSTER'S LAW</u>
<u>A PORTRAIT IN ASH AND LACE</u>

ABOUT THE AUTHOR

Sofia Aves writes fast-paced police romances, suspenseful mysteries, steamy cowboys with a Montana backdrop and the occasional cheeky god. She loves reading Indie authors and hides her collection of college romance books beneath an ever-growing TBR pile.

Sofia is a mum of three crazies and an overly large fur baby who thinks she's a teacup puppy. She loves orchids but can't always keep them alive. Sofia lives near Brisbane, Australia.

www.sofiaves.com

Join Sofia's newsletter & get a free Blue Blooded Brothers short story:

https://BookHip.com/CNMQFX

Follow Sofia on BookBub:

https://www.bookbub.com/profile/sofia-aves?follw=true

CONTENTS

Copyright © Sofia Aves 2021..II

CONTENTS VII

PROLOGUE 1

CHAPTER ONE 3

CHAPTER TWO 21

CHAPTER THREE..31

CHAPTER FOUR..39

CHAPTER FIVE...51

CHAPTER SIX..61

CHAPTER SEVEN..81

CHAPTER EIGHT 103

CHAPTER NINE 129

CHAPTER TEN 147

CHAPTER ELEVEN 165

EPILOGUE...179

ACKNOWLEDGEMENTS...193

ABOUT THE AUTHOR..195

Read Sofia's Series..197

PROLOGUE

I wasn't always a clean-shaven sharpshooter. In fact, growing up as an army brat to a Special Forces Dad, I was a royal pain in the ass to everyone I interacted with. Hours spent with spray paint cans at the back of the fields on the base where I wasn't supposed to be in the first place while Dad worked. I entertained myself with discarded ordnance shells and making keyrings for imaginary mates from used ammo.

My childhood.

It was as far removed from *normal* as anything could possibly be. No mother, because she left shortly after Dad returned from the desert with a shiny, albeit destructive, new aspect of PTSD. Deployment life wasn't conducive to family life, though I watched other kids play with two parents with ill-disguised envy.

Those imaginary mates from every army base around the country became real mates as I grew into my teenage years; junior officers and younger troops wanting to show off their knowledge to someone who understood.

Because I *did* understand.

I lived the life with them, the few weeks of the year the unit spent at home; watched them train, read their tech and procedural manuals.

Until I became one of them.

CHAPTER ONE

KING

My mark wore a pink and black chequered tie that clashed horribly with his date's dress. She, at least, exuded a dash of class. Even from my perch at the top of the residential block opposite the high end restaurant, I could see that.

My hands gripped at air, missing the familiar shape of my rifle, but I was under strict orders to leave it at home.

I could have as easily parted with my legs.

"Nothing." Scotty 'Joker' Evans rocked back onto his heels, jiggling about. Ever struggling with the serious side of our work, we could always rely on a smart ass comment from him in the midst of gunfire. Hence, his callsign.

We had all earned them, in one form or another.

"Sit still, you old bastard," I groused. "Don't they teach you anything useful in the RAF?"

"Piss off, King. You might actually learn something if you shut up once in a while." His British accent thickening, Joker gave me his trademark grin, one that many a lady—both young and not so young—dropped their knickers for.

I snorted softly, turning my attention back to the politician and his date. After his pedicure, he met her at his regular restaurant, not far from the expensive suite someone else rented for him.

The man wasn't influential yet, but he had the potential, which put him squarely on our radar.

Find out everything you can about him and file it for that rainy day when you'll need to use it.

Anything to protect the nation, even if it was several oceans away and twenty years in advance.

Joker continued to grumble beside me.

The politician—I winced again at his horrendous taste in ties—rose, tossing his napkin to the floor with disdain.

I zoomed in on my helmet display, studying her face, and then his. Had he hit her up for the night and she said no? He definitely misread that one.

His date folded her arms, looking away from him as a herd of waiters congregated about them. Even from the top of the next building, their fussing was overly pronounced.

I wondered if they were as keen to get Ugly Tie out of the restaurant as his date clearly intended.

A woman at the table behind turned to study the commotion, and I nearly dropped my kit.

Stunner.

Heavy lashes and dark, wavy chestnut hair were distinctly out of place in an exclusive restaurant in Cambodia. I shook my head, mentally tracing over her toned figure tucked into something red and sparkly.

Not the time or place, King.

My mark moved the fastest he had in weeks, and naturally I wasn't even watching him. He stormed through the restaurant's doors that were held open for him, the doormen bowing low. He sank into a car waiting at the curb, despite the fact his rented residence was only a three-block walk.

I tapped the radio at my side.

"Ugly Tie incoming. Same as usual." I smirked. It wasn't the first time my mark had left a date, though it *was* the first time she had kicked *him* out. I suspected his not-so-sweet talking skills had something to do with it. Or maybe he had terrible bedroom eyes.

"...the fuck? Reception's shit. Bald Eagle? ...moving?"

I snuffled a laugh. "Yeah. That one. See you back at the block."

"Don't go changing designators over the radio, man." Lincon Kelly—*Ace*—berated me as soon as I stepped through the door of the holiday unit. The small section of Z-Unit cramped into a space that should have held four teenagers on schoolies at the absolute most.

Instead, three highly-trained military operatives hand-picked from their careers were stuffed into it, though technically, none of us existed on paper any more.

Wires and parts of computers lay in a haphazard mess strewn across the entire combined lounge and living area, surrounding the oversized mass of muscle planted in the centre.

"Fuck, it's like walking into Beruit." I stepped gingerly over some cords I thought weren't as critical and trod on some that were. Hearts moved and I flinched. "Seriously. Can't we look at these people before we name them? Ugly Tie is so much better than Bald fucking Eagle."

"We're naming *us* or anything that matters." Joker laid our surveillance kit on the table in a clatter of tech that hadn't been packed up properly.

"Damn, man." My flinch became a wince. "Will Mr Politician be replaced by the next gung-ho politician when he runs out of cash or sponsors? Yes. Will he run out of dates due to social ineptness? Also yes. Don't you ever feel sorry for these bastards?" I retraced my steps and claimed the bags of tech before Joker could damage anything further.

"You want me to feel sorry for a rich prick who bleeds poor people dry so he can live his rich prick lifestyle?" Hearts glared at me over his shoulder, pointing back the way I had come. "Plug that one back in. Talk about pricks," he muttered, tapping away frantically.

"How long do we keep tailing Ugly Tie?" Joker asked softly, running a hand through his hair.

I grinned. "I knew it would catch on."

"Seriously. The worst thing these local people do is poach from wildlife reserves because they're starving." Joker stuffed his hands into his pockets. "That's not a crime."

"Hell. You are in a mood."

"We've been here too long."

"You're a pair of whiny bitches. We're out in three days. Two more on recon, then we catch our flight home." Hearts shook his head, the behemoth of a man leaning forward, reading data from four screens at once.

"Home, man." Joker cheersed me with his water bottle.

I downed mine, and headed for the bedrooms.

"Where are you going?" Scotty called after me.

"I need to run."

Ignoring grumbles from the other two, I retreated into my spartan room and tugged off my protective vest, stripping back to bare skin. The kevlar didn't weigh much—and every one of us trained hundreds of hours wearing it—that it felt more naked without it than in it.

Every muscle had tightened with too many hours of surveillance. The inactivity killed me, in more ways than one, but at least I wasn't as fidgety as Joker. I trotted down the fire escape stairs, jumping the last few steps to hit the ground running.

Twenty blocks later, I turned around. Those same, tight muscles burning, I sprinted for as long as I could hold it before dropping back to a jog. The run wasn't just to keep my body going; the muscle that needed the most work was my brain.

Being cramped into a hotel room for nearly three months with only basic surveillance work came close to crippling me. My two hours out each night ate into my allocated sleep time, but my brain—and my body—were grateful for it.

Every inch of my body burned by the time I hit the fire escape for the return journey, my lungs sucking at air that wouldn't fill them as I sprinted the final flight.

The rest of my unit was already down by the time I crept back into the room.

Two days never seemed so long. Ugly Tie did his usual rounds both mornings, collecting his coffee and blow job from the delivery girl he under tipped for her tenacity and service under duress. Lunch was a simple affair involving lots of booze and too many associates who sat close together so there was no room for anyone to stab them in the back.

Dinner and another failed date.

On the second night, Ugly Tie stayed in.

"That's unusual." Hearts was still tapping at his keyboards in the apartment. "Stay with him, make sure nothing changes. Don't blow this on our last night. I'm keen to be on home soil." He punctuated his last words with a harsh tap.

Both Joker and I winced at the spliced static assailing our ears.

"He'd better do nothing." I adjusted the settings on my visor, but it didn't give me any greater insight on my mark.

"He's made two calls, hasn't eaten, and now..." Joker trailed off, squinting as he repeated my process, "he's going to bed? The hussies have worn him out."

"We're done, then." I stretched my calf slowly; the thing had gone to sleep beneath me.

We packed up in silence from then until we hit the street, the local night markets still active. Joker checked over his shoulder as he stepped out onto the street, jerking backward in a hurry as a tuk-tuk tore past him, a retro beatbox pounding in his wake.

"Hell, you do need to go home." I laughed as he cursed.

"Yeah, well. Home isn't home, is it?" he snapped cryptically, his cultured British accent thickening with his irritation. Finding a break in the traffic, he jogged across the road, leaving me on the other side.

The months we spent out of the country cost us plenty, but even so, none of us really had the lives others might expect. A regular special ops soldier might not be permitted to talk about his work, but to the rest of the world, Z Boys didn't exist.

Heading home did sound good, but Joker was right; we were headed for Australian soil. His home was halfway across the globe.

I inhaled my last few hours of Cambodia, relishing the lights and never-ceasing life of the place.

"Any chance you two can keep up?" Heart grunted as we headed for a small and inconsequential airfield.

Situated a few blocks from our hotel, it gave us a chance to hop onto a local charter and onto another, smaller plane to eventually land on military soil for our flight home.

Customs saw soldiers ready to head home, manifests provided from our cover unit dated months ago, and the pilots saw a pretty piece of paper with our false records, which they ignored.

"You make it sound like you're struggling, old man." I grinned at the big man's back, knowing he'd probably kick my ass the next time we trained together.

Which would probably be the day after we touched down on home ground.

Hearts had a good decade on me in skills and training, but my determination to push all his buttons equaled that.

"Just keep moving." Joker loped by me, his longer strides eating mine.

"Taking the order to *blend in* a little much, aren't you?"

The tall man's shoulders sloped, his back slightly bent, though his pack weighed little. Each of us had been in our civvies for so long, I knew it had begun to impact our mindset. Uniform was part of the training, part of the conditioning that kept us strong, focused.

I wondered if Joker remembered how to march. Ace would kick our backsides into gear in a few days.

We left the monotonous drone of the main streets behind, pushing through the outskirts of the town. Joker disappeared into foliage ahead, the track marked by a well-trodden patch of mud that disappeared between two trees.

A shadow passed across it, then another.

I frowned; neither were big enough to be one of my boys. Jogging the last few steps, I sloshed through the mud, a new drone filling my ears from the front. But the shadows disappeared across the foliage, not into the airfield beyond.

A handful of lean-to huts stood off to one side in a clearing, their occupants flitting about with menial, day-to-day tasks. A tiny figure darted into a hut, followed by a head of dark, chestnut waves.

My frown deepened. I glanced back to where Hearts and Joker had disappeared, but something drew me toward the lean-to.

Swearing softly, I slid the zip on my backpack, digging in to find my sidearm. I held it at my hip, fumbling with my other hand for the magazine.

The tiny hut was even tinier from the doorway. People scattered as I approached. Inside, a long-haired woman dressed in dark jeans and a rumpled tee huddled on the dirt floor in a hunched ball, talking quickly but soothingly to the shadow of a child I saw earlier. A satchel strung across her chest as she gestured to the child too fast for me to dechiper their conversation.

A knot grew in my stomach as I realised they weren't alone. Money slipped from her hand to the child, who disappeared across the other side of the house and out through a window.

The woman turned to face the only other occupant, a man holding a matte black submachine gun aimed at her. He made a gesture with one hand, but she shook her head, clutching the strap of her laptop bag strung across her chest.

"At louy," she said in a clear voice.

No money.

I blinked. Reacting calmly in a shitty situation didn't come naturally to most people. It was something trained into your brain as you weighed the options in front of you with a clear assessment of what the outcome of each action would be.

Standing in the shadow outside the man's line of sight, I loaded my weapon and took another look at her.

I need to know who you are.

The ability to do that probably came down to how I dealt with the threat before me. In a darkened space on the outskirts of town, this was only going to end one way, and for the woman, it just came down to how messy the outcome was.

"She doesn't have any money." I held my arm just slightly behind me, as though reaching out to comfort her, edging into the hut. "You saw her give it away."

Large eyes swung my way, but I gave every inch of my attention to the man demanding it.

"I don't want her money." The man's English was better than I expected.

"Good. You hop out of here, honey," I said softly, flicking my finger behind my back.

Those eyes widened in my peripheral vision. The moment she began to move, I knew it was a shithouse idea to try to remove her from the situation she had gotten herself into without creating a greater threat than I could offer.

"Stay. Please." The man's cordial words were disputed by the jiggling of his weapon. A second armed man appeared from the other side of the hut—from a rear door, I assumed, since he didn't use the window the child had. Probably *why* the child had used the window as her exit strategy. This day was getting better and better.

I tried hard not to wince. "I need to take her home," I said firmly, sidestepping across the woman.

The tip of the gun followed my movement. Objective achieved.

More movement from the side of the hut I had entered from, but this time they were familiar shadows, which gave me additional options.

"She stays. Fun times." The man smiled.

I wished he hadn't. Several teeth were missing from it.

It was a moral choice on two fronts which may or may not have been altruistic. Save the girl, and fight the fight, because that was what we were trained for. And with his weapon aimed at me, I had a hall pass for what came next.

A simple aim and depression of the trigger.

And called that fateful word that would bring us all together.

I dropped to one knee.

"Contact."

CHAPTER TWO

CHRISSY

Bullets flew around the room, gunfire echoing between my ears in a hollow way inside the small building. I had no idea if they were aimed at my head or not, because my head appeared to be covered by an enormous hand that pushed me toward the hard-packed ground.

Boots slapped the earthen floor in front of me, a herd of giants stampeding around us. With the amount of dirt the men scuffed up in their boots as they shuffled about, it lent a surreal ambience to the situation.

Maybe I can add this to my blog.

Or maybe I wouldn't. If I got shot, that was. Someone else could write that one up. My site was always bugging me to get more insurance, but I didn't believe in it. Though right now, insurance seemed like a rather big thing.

Stupid, stupid, stupid.

I knew better than to give help to a child in need, especially one asking for food, medical assistance or money. But regardless of what my head said, I couldn't let a little girl starve. But then, that got me right here, with her.

My head ran in a hundred different directions at once, none of them particularly useful.

Hands scuffed beneath my arms, dragging me forward and sideways.

"What're we—" I gasped into his palm, seeing enough to know he pulled me into another, smaller room before he shoved my head back to where it had been before.

The golden, lean-muscled god, stuffing my head in his crotch.

Could you die of such a thing?

Am I high?

Distant retorts rang a staccato beat around the small hut. The man's body heat pulsed over me, his grip firm but gentle around the back of my head. He shifted, the hard ridge of his zipper and what lay beneath roughly grazing my lips.

In response, I stuck my tongue out and sluiced it sideways over the length of what I thought was his denim-covered cock. I was pleased when he let out a long, stifled groan.

"Dear God, woman, are you right?" His Aussie accent rippled around me, sexy as hell, and reminded me of home.

"You put me here," I muttered, ending up with a mouthful of material, which jerked between my words.

"Didn't you think it was a stupid idea to follow a kid into a house where you didn't know them?" He fired another shot. The hand on the back of my head gentled, but he didn't let me up.

"I didn't think this would happen," I gasped, instinctually flattening against the warm body providing me protection as more shots rang out deafeningly in the small space.

"You didn't think?" he asked, his question laced with disbelief.

"Well, I knew the risks, but I couldn't let a clearly malnourished child wander the streets on her own."

"It didn't occur to you that maybe that kid should be at school?"

I paused, unwilling to answer him. "Well—"

"It didn't, did it?" I could hear the smile in his voice.

What sort of man laughs in the middle of a freaking gunfight?

His stomach moved with suppressed laughter. I nuzzled a little deeper into the material around my head cheekily, more than a little light-headed.

"While you're down there—" His voice came out strained. Another shot fired, and his hand moved to my shoulder as he called something else out. "You're taking this awful well for a girl who's probably never been shot at before."

The world shifted around me. We were moving across the floor and outside the hut before I had my feet pressed to solid ground properly.

"Move, you ugly bastards," the man shouted, clutching me to his chest like a giant football.

"Talk to your mumma about that one, kid," a man with a British accent flung back, laughter teasing the edge of a cultured voice.

These men are insane.

I only had time to process a single thought before we burst out into the open. Fresh air hit me in the face.

Sunlight warmed my icy skin as I stumbled on the soft ground. I pressed my hands to my knees as my lungs seemed to suck air into themselves all on their own. My world stopped spinning as a pair of well-loved combat boots appeared in my vision. I straightened, my thanks caught in my throat.

Startling sapphire eyes stared down into mine.

Down, because the man who talked me through my first gunfight was a giant. He stood at least six-and-a-half feet tall, with shoulders that could have withstood the weight of the world. Remembering how fast he came to the aid of a stranger, I wondered if perhaps he did.

My head barely came up to the centre of his chest. I broke my gaze from those incredible eyes to discover the rest of the man I had developed intimate knowledge of within a few minutes.

His hand dropped to his belt, his thumb brushing the denim beneath. The outline of him was clear, the fabric straining around him.

I ached to feel him against my lips again.

Is my mouth watering?

Where the hell is my head at?

He took a step closer, the hand lifting from his belt.

I followed its movement, the ground moving with me. "Just a minute." I held up a hand, but it moved, too.

"*Shit,*" he swore, calling out to someone.

I missed what else was happening, because I was busy bent at the waist, spewing last night's splurge dinner over my spotless Diamond Light Jimmy Choo's.

Voices muttered behind me, but I gave up trying to decipher words. Everything shook as I straightened. A water bottle appeared beneath my chin, paired with a handful of crumpled tissues.

"Go easy on the water, babe." Sirens wailed in the near distance. "I mean, take your time, but hurry up."

"Why?" I sipped the water and burped softly into my hand, nearly passing out at my breath. "Do you have somewhere else to be?"

"Actually, yeah." The words cut off sharply.

I looked up and, for the first time, I became aware of the people around us. Two men knelt with their hands cuffed behind their backs. I recognised both from the shadows of the hut, a shiver wracking me. I would see those faces in my dreams. Their weapons sat at a distance, dismantled.

Two more men in regular clothing surveyed the area with a professional eye that reeked of a military bearing as they talked softly between themselves.

"You're what, Army?" I asked, the pieces falling into place for me. More than just Army, because these guys really were the *best you can be* type they advertised for.

A crooked grin split across his face. "Something like that." His hand came down on my back, stroking a gentle pattern. "You gonna be okay?"

"You really do have to go?" I asked, panic rising in me at the thought of having to deal with the fall out from what had happened alone.

Oh, hell, I have to explain to the police what happened.

In another country.

A travel blogger of four years plus eighty-three countries and counting, I had never been in this situation before. Or anything even close to it.

My lungs sucked at the air again, but it appeared to have evacuated from where I stood.

"Okay, honey." He wound his hands around my shoulders, crouching to put me at shoulder-level with him. "You're tough as hell. You'll be okay." He kissed the back of my head tenderly, holding my hair back from my face.

You're perfect.

And I'm in hell.

"I'm good," I lied, hoping to hell I convinced someone, because that level of transparency boded poorly for the next few hours. I didn't want to know what the inside of a police station looked like in Cambodia.

"You're good," he confirmed, tilting my head back.

Gentle fingers tidied up the corners of my mouth, tucked strands of hair behind my ears. Out of nowhere, he produced mints, slipping two between my lips before I could argue. He leaned in, one arm tight around my shoulders like a steel support. "I wish this had been any other day. We were never here. Make something up."

Lips grazed my ear, and he was gone.

Suddenly familiar combat boots were replaced by a scuffed, utilitarian lace-up pair of police-issue.

His warmth faded from my body long after he had gone.

CHAPTER THREE

KING

The feel of her lips pressed over my jeans haunted me for the seven hours and ten minutes it took to put us back on Australian soil.

The C17 hit the Cairns runway with its usual bump. I slid my custom-cut piece of foam out from beneath my asscheek as the cargo plane slowed, resisting the urge to rub circulation back into it.

"Good to be home," Joker grinned.

"Yeah, good." I echoed.

"Hell, man. Are you still pining about her? Go get yourself a tourist to wash her off."

There was no washing her off. She'd had her perfect mouth wrapped around my dick and I hadn't even asked her name.

You need to forget her.

I'd been trying for the last seven hours, locked in my own hell with only her memory for company.

"Yeah, right after Ace lets us out to play." I ran my hand over my head. "Debriefing this will be shite."

Beside me, Hearts snorted.

His eyes stayed forward, though his hands moved in a familiar pattern. He took a phantom of his holstered pistol apart between his hands, then put it back together. Every movement precise, his fingers curved around a hard surface that wasn't actually there.

Heart's breath matched each action, the repetitive motion better than any therapy they gave us at ground level.

"So much time to screw with his head." Joker laced his hands behind his head, the epitome of relaxation. Nothing appeared to faze the man, despite having fired his weapon only minutes before we managed to clamber on board our secure transport out of a country we weren't supposed to be in.

An image of a head in my lap covered everything around me. Chestnut curls and dark eyes peeking from beneath black lashes turned up to me filled my vision. I cursed inwardly. There was no chance in hell I would be able to function if I couldn't forget the woman I'd held beneath a hail of bullets.

Hours after the event, her ghost remained at my side.

I wished I could take the memory of her apart and put it back together the way Hearts did with his imaginary weapon.

"If I call this self-defence, then someone will end up lying on the stand." Lincoln 'Ace' Kelly glared across his wide desk. He dropped his head into one hand, running the other over his short, regulation haircut. "You keep doing this to me and I'll spend so much time with the brass, I'll know them better than their wives."

"You are the brass. Sir," I added, gesturing to the ever growing collection of medals decorating the Major's chest.

Ace sent me a dark look. "You have no idea the paperwork that's gone into saving your ass from going before the high commision, King. What would your father think of that?"

I wouldn't fucking know any more.

It wasn't like I'd had the chance to talk to him recently. He'd passed while I was on deployment, and I'd gotten the message from a friend who used to work with him. The military grapevine at its finest.

I completed the mission and went straight back to work. There had been no reason to return to the shithole house at the bottom end of the country when we'd been estranged for years.

I swallowed, gripping my fingers tight behind my back and lost the battle to keep my shoulders relaxed. "Sorry, Sir."

"Damn right you're sorry. Get me your reports done and sign your weapons in with one of the Tran boys."

"Yes, Sir." I saluted by rote, spinning on my heel.

"Lieutenant? Good job on spotting the incident in the first place." Ace's head went back to the paperwork covering his desk.

I grinned as I left his office, his few words the highest praise he would give.

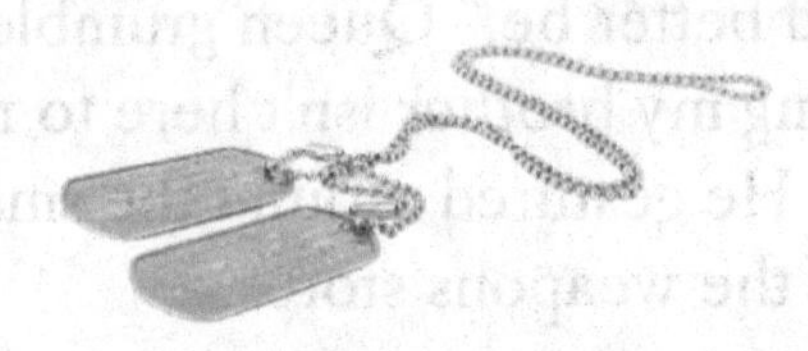

"Did you dig it into the dirt?" Queen bitched as he dismantled my weapon and began cleaning it.

"Dirt? Hell no— ah, yeah. There was a dirt wall. Might have shot around it." I pushed the sign in sheet back across the small window he spent a lot of his time at.

"Or through it." Ryker Tran—Queen to the rest of us—shot me a filthy look, drawing himself up to his all of five-foot ten-inch height, and looking for all the world the epitome of his call sign. Black hair that was not a regulation cut flopped over one side.

His twin brother didn't raise his head from where he sat at a long table behind Queen, the weapons we had returned with scattered around him. A filthy rag was wrapped around his hand, a bottle of oil sat to one side of him.

"That, too." A small pile of dust dribbled out of the barrel that disgusted even me. "Sorry, man."

"You'd better be," Queen grumbled. "Good thing my brother isn't here to rip you a new one." He gestured around the small interior of the weapons store.

An assortment of weapons and pouches filled the bench tables behind him, each with their paperwork nestled neatly beneath.

"I can help," I offered, reaching for the door to Queen's domain.

He raised a hand without looking up. "No need. If you don't screw with my system, I don't need to bitch slap you."

I snorted; Ryker Tran's equivalent of a bitch slap would knock even Ace on his ass. The man specialised in martial arts and hand-to-hand combat. If things went sideways in close quarters during an operation, there was no one I'd prefer beside me than the Tran twins.

"I'm out." I jogged back to the block, aiming for the showers and a change of clothes. I probably still had Cambodia stuck to me, and while I liked the place, it reminded me only of the woman whose name I'd chosen not to ask.

I took the stairs two at a time, my boot heels ringing an echo up the concrete staircase. The industrial carpet of my floor was familiar beneath my feet. Hearts exited the showers room as I kicked my own door open.

"Ran you out of hot water," he called, striding back to his room wearing only a towel.

I rolled my eyes, commenting loudly enough for him to hear.

"Ass."

CHAPTER FOUR

KING

Pink hibiscus warred with a lurid, lime-green background across my chest as we walked through customs for our flight.

"We're gonna be late," muttered Queen, taking twice as many steps as the rest of us to keep up. "I hate being late."

"At least we won't lose King." His twin brother, Kai Tran, aka Knave, laughed, slapping my back too hard.

"Keep your fucking hands to yourself, Knave," I groused.

My day-glo shirt had been selected from a pile Ace had deposited on the lunch tables, alongside a short description of our mission. Local fishing boats hadn't returned, and there were rumours across the ocean of something bigger than sea monsters

"Buck's party in Tonga. Fishing trip. Make it lary."

He'd stood back and watched while the twins went at it, digging through until they extracted matching red shirts. Hearts had picked a shirt covered in martini glasses filled with pin-up girls.

But the pièce de résistance of our showcase was a spectacular specimen of a shirt that Joker had scrounged out of the selection. A cowboy dressed only in hot pants rode a bucking shark that spewed a rainbow into the ocean that splayed across his chest.

If nothing else, we would be memorable.

And right now, that was exactly what we were meant to be.

"Not sure what you're gonna rope, but I'd keep my eyes on those in case they take to your hotpants," Hearts nudged Joker in the ribs with a not-so-friendly elbow.

The tallest Tongan I had ever seen walked through Cairns International Terminal, holiday goers scattering in his path.

Joker huffed, faking a glare. "I mean, I'm not saying I wouldn't, but..." His gaze zeroed in obviously on a woman in blue jeans and a mop of chestnut curls that bounced almost to the waist, "but I have my sights set a little lower."

The Tran boys latched onto that one. Scotty joined in mercilessly. But the terminal swirled around me in a wave, and two short steps later, my hand was on the woman's shoulder, my heart in my throat as she turned.

Pale blue eyes unsuited to the orangy fake tan stained skin stared back at me.

"Sorry. Thought you were someone else," I muttered, backing away and bumped into the mountain of flesh and muscle that was Hearts.

He patted my ass. "Sorry, boy, you're not my type."

"But I kiss so well." I shoved at him with a quick grin, banter falling from my lips.

We hadn't left the airport yet, and already the personas Ace had given us settled over our own; the party boys out for one last shebang.

"Seven hours of this. Are you fucking kidding me?" Queen grumbled, poking at the broken screen in the back of the seat before him.

A small child rose over the back of it, blowing a raspberry that covered the three seats behind him in toddler spit.

I couldn't hold back laughter as the Tran boys and Joker swiped their faces clean, the mother audibly dressing her child down in front of us.

"Why did I get the bitch seat?" Joker muttered, nodding to where he was pinned between the twins.

I grinned over Ryker's head. "What, you didn't want to sit with the footy team Hearts has going on?" I jerked my head backward.

Behind us, Hearts had been happy with the back row of the plane all to himself—until the big Tongan we spotted earlier brought eleven of his friends with him. Each larger and more jovial than the next, Hearts had been subject to several albums of family photos, eventually being included in some of his very own.

Joker snuffed a laugh. "Family, man. At least they have it."

His eyes fell closed, his head back in the epitome of calm in a sea of noise, but I'd worked with Scotty Evans for long enough to recognise his resting *fuck off* face.

Nodding to myself, I flicked through the working menu on my own screen, settling on *The Mandalorian.*

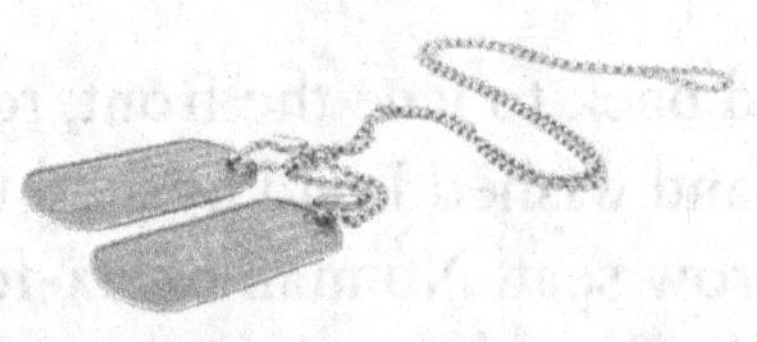

Seven hours wasn't a long flight for any of us; each Z Boy had been on longer trips to the desert and plenty of other places we weren't supposed to be in. Combined with a hundred personal sweat issues while crammed into cattle class, the cargo hold of a C17 no longer looked so bad.

"I'm never doing this again," Hearts grunted, extracting himself from the row he was stuffed into, popping into the aisle suddenly. The hostess passing him leapt sideways with a small shriek. "Shit. Sorry, love," he gave an endearing grin, but paired with his lary shirt, a red face and a string of plastic frangipanis around his neck, it missed the mark.

A crinkled, older lady in the seat opposite shushed him without bothering to remove her headphones.

"You're doing a fine job," I laughed at him.

Hearts growled at me, edging his way toward the amenities.

I turned back to face the front, rolling tight shoulders, and wished I had pushed the Major for an exit row seat. No man of six-foot, five-inches height should ever be jammed into a small space. Not if he wanted to use his knees again.

A few rows in front, a woman raised her arms over her head. I grinned, watching them arch over the top of her seat. At least I wasn't alone in my discomfort.

Until she rose, sliding into the aisle. Glossy, dark waves tumbled down her back to accentuate the tiny waist and generous curves I last saw wobbling unsteadily as I told her I had to leave her at the mercy of the local police and prayed she got her ass out of trouble.

"What are the odds?" Joker asked softly over Queen's head.

I turned too fast, a sharp pain pairing with a crunching noise I hoped was only audible in my ears.

From the look on Joker's face, it wasn't.

"How long have you known?" I demanded, scrubbing the back of my neck. A soft fragrance, both fresh and heavy at once, wafted over me. I gripped the armrest, still holding Joker's gaze.

"Since we got on the plane. You were too busy giving us shit." He leaned back into his prior position, closing his eyes.

She passed by us, but I didn't look back at her. Not yet.

"Were you going to tell me?"

Joker shook his head without opening his eyes. "I hadn't decided."

Asshole.

"Fine." I pushed up, tensing my legs, but my knees worked the way they were supposed to, even after hours squashed in the seat. Mostly. I joined my mystery woman in the lineup for the toilet. "Hey," I murmured familiarly to her back, leaning a little closer than I probably should have.

The little old lady who had told Hearts off watched me with a speculative glint in her eye. I got the feeling that if I did anything inappropriate, Granny would be the one to dish out social justice.

"Hi—" She turned, reacting automatically, but the brown eyes that widened beneath thick lashes had nothing programmed about it. "Oh, my god. I never—I should have—wait, how dare you?" Her soft hiss grew a little.

Beside us, the granny lifted a solid looking handbag onto her lap.

I hoped she didn't have a taser. Or OC spray.

"Good to see you, too." I leaned one arm against the bulkhead above her as the line shifted forward a step, boxing her into me.

"I mean—" she faltered. My mystery woman closed her eyes and took a deep breath. When she opened them again, confusion crossed her face.

"I should have gotten your name. Made sure you were alright. Afterward." I smiled, aching to run my eyes over her body. I held her gaze instead.

The deep brown of her eyes were flecked with green, spearing into the centre. It was like looking into the depths of a rainforest, filled with secrets I needed to uncover.

"Yes. You should have," she said tartly, though her smile undermined the sharp tone in her voice. "I'm not sure I said thank you. Did I?"

"I honestly don't remember." I shrugged. "I got the gist of that, though." Even her scent reminded me of a rainforest: fresh rain and earthy scents mingling in a heady concoction that went straight to my dick.

"Well, thank you. Um—" She stalled and frowned.

"Noah King." I smiled, tracing her lips with my gaze, though I wanted to follow them with my fingers. The tip of her pink tongue slipped between the seam, wetting her bottom lip. I watched with fascination, gripping the bulkhead with straining fingers.

Kissing her in the loo line of an aircraft is inappropriate.

That, and the little lady who sat next to me might tase me in the ass if I got all predatory on the girl.

"Chrissy." My mystery girl saved me from my own private hell, grinning as though she knew what had been going through my head.

"How come you keep turning up wherever I am, Chrissy?" I caught one of her curls, winding it loosely around my finger. The silky lock turned smoothly, sliding along my finger.

Chrissy looked like she had stopped breathing.

"I'm a travel blogger," she blurted, expelling a laugh on a gusty breath. "Okay. You have got to stop that." She tugged her hair free, repeating the process I had with her own fingers.

"Stop what?" I eased a little closer, noting most of the line had moved on.

Granny watched us from the corner of her eye.

"Stop making me feel like we're the only two people in the room," she murmured softly.

The air stalled between us as her gaze dropped to my lips, her head tilting back a little.

Dipping my head down to her, I leaned in closer, but that was as far as I got before a shock caught me in the thigh.

I hit the floor of the plane without knocking anyone about, looking with no small degree of shock at the granny, who had jabbed me with what looked an awful lot like a cattle prod.

CHAPTER FIVE

CHRISSY

Miss Katherine was a trained dominatrix who took on a vigilante side with young women. Which included me when she saw Noah chatting me up, and decided he was doing it all wrong.

Our disturbance had also caught the attention of the air marshal, who had a quiet word with Noah while he was prostrate on the floor.

"Thank you." I smiled, taking the small jar of balm with a smile, laughter threatening to overwhelm me.

Noah rubbed his leg, a wary look in his eyes. "Glad you didn't go any higher," he muttered, pushing himself off the floor. "And damn lucky I was wearing jeans."

"It makes up for your taste in shirts, young man. Any higher and you'd be no use to her at all." Miss Katherine clucked her tongue, apparently unintimidated by the huge man who towered over everyone seated in economy.

"How did you get that through security?" Noah asked, nodding to the zapper which retracted neatly into itself and was stowed into her massive purse.

I wondered what else she had inside it.

"A lady has the right to self defence." Miss Katherine zipped her bag up, then motioned Noah closer, a conspiratorial look on her face. She cupped her hand around his ear and said in a far too-loud stage whisper, "I taught him how to do a proper cavity search."

Barely holding back my own laughter, I watched Noah's sexy-ass face turn an interesting shade of red.

The air marshall shook his head, resuming his seat on the other side of the plane.

"Come on." I pulled Noah away from Miss Katherine. "I have a spare seat next to me."

"You're not going to attack me with a fork or anything, are you?" he asked jokingly, but a new wariness lit his eyes.

"No, I'm not going to attack you." I giggled, sliding across to the window seat and turned my back to the wall of the plane.

I tucked one leg beneath me, kicking my shoes off, and watched Noah fold himself into the small space. Blond stubble covered his shaven head, his deep, golden tan only serving to accentuate the deep sea blue of his eyes. Eyes that held an endless reservoir of laughter in them, despite what I knew he was capable of doing.

Noah King.

Now I had a name for the man I had been fantasizing about for three weeks.

Every time I closed my eyes, I tasted the denim-and-sweat musky flavour that was uniquely him. Felt his hand on the back of my head, holding me protectively, but sexy as all get out at the same time. But then always back to those eyes as he said he had to leave after saving me.

Those same laughing eyes that surveyed me now.

"You left me in a hell of a mess, you know." I poked his knee with my bare toe.

"I got you out of the helluva mess that *you* got yourself into," he countered.

"You're not telling me you're on a holiday. I saw your friends," I reminded him, nodding back toward where he had been seated.

"Buck's party," he said, his mouth curling up at the edges a little, though the smile didn't make it to his eyes.

"Liar." I poked him, but the evasion didn't bother me as much as I thought it might. He—*they*—clearly were Army, or part of some military organisation. Hell, the lot of them could have been the Army on their own. If he wouldn't tell me what he was doing, then it wasn't my place to pry.

"Probably," he agreed. "Why aren't you in business class? I would have thought a travel blogger," he gestured at the cramped space around us, "would be off the cattle-class list for a critic."

"Not that good or that famous," I said ruefully, smiling back.

"Pity," he murmured. One long, muscular arm stretched across the back of my seat, his fingers tangling into my hair.

"Uh no," I pretended to recoil, biting my tongue lightly to prevent the laughter from bubbling out of me.

"What is it?" To his credit, Noah didn't move away.

"This." I tugged at the sleeve of his island-themed shirt, tracing one bright pink flower with my fingertip. I made no pretence about exploring the muscle concealed beneath. A flamingo materialised from the fabric, hiding amongst the flowers. It gave me another good reason to study him. "It's absolutely hideous."

"Ah. Maybe I should lose it then." His arm retracted and he began to unbutton his shirt with speed.

"You wouldn't," I gasped, reaching out to pull the material back together before the hostess raised hell over public nudity.

"I would." Noah's hands dropped to catch my wrists when he reached the last button, suddenly closer than he had been before. He slid my hands inside the thin cotton, pressing them to the sculpted muscle beneath. "Better?" he asked in a low voice.

"Much." I swallowed, pressing my palms flat over the heat of his skin. Peeling each frozen finger back, I traced the planes of flesh he offered up. "Uh— I've never done this. Hook up with a stranger on a plane." Noah edged a little closer, the air between us charged in the still before a storm. Like the one currently swirling in his eyes that was so tempting to fall into. "A mile high club virgin?"

I bit my lip and nodded. "Afraid so. It's sort of the fairytale, to meet a hot stranger on a plane and...you know. But it never comes true. Right?" I didn't know if I was rambling to him or myself.

"Is that what we're doing? Fulfilling your fantasies?"

"I'm curerntly groping you, so..." I raised a shoulder but made no move to pull back from him. Plus, he felt too good under my hands.

"And Miss Katherine has given you plenty of material for your blog." He grinned, stretching his arm back to where it had been before, his fingers winding through my hair to stroke the back of my neck.

My laugh died in my throat at the incredibly intimate caress. Maybe it wouldn't be with anyone else, but somehow, Noah blocked out the rest of the world for me, and it wasn't just his bulk.

"True," I whispered, frozen between leaning back into his touch where he massaged my neck or leaning closer to him. I pressed my hands over finely carved pecs as a compromise, and to hide the tremor in them.

"Done with exploration time?" He swirled his fingers at the base of my neck, the crooked corner of his mouth the only indication he gave.

"Well—"

Noah's hand curved completely around my neck, pulling me into him. "Want to become a member?" His mouth brushed mine as he spoke.

I shook my head, goosebumps erupting over my skin as his hand tightened the tiniest amount.

"No." I squeaked the word.

Wasn't this what every travel fantasy contained? A hot-as-hades passenger with a proposition in a semi-public space—especially with a man I had been fantasizing every which way about for the past weeks since I had last seen him.

So why was I absolutely terrified of where this was going?

The storm in his eyes took on a darker shade as his mouth covered mine, holding me there for an instant.

I leaned into him with a sigh, sliding my hands over his abs, tracing each ridge of muscle with my fingertips.

Noah's breath shattered against my mouth, his tongue stoking along my bottom lip as he tilted my head back, and deepened the kiss when I leaned into him. Noah's kisses became faster, indecent for anywhere around other people.

Heat rushed through my chest, heading south in a languid pace that kept me on edge.

Or he did. Hell, what would sex be like withhits man, if this was how he kissed?

"Noah, I haven't— I can't—" I stuttered against his mouth, drawing back, only to be pulled deeper into him.

My head swirled with desire that overrode any sensibility I might have retained, I stroked lower over his carved abs, tracing across the line at the top of his jeans, over the familiar shape beneath my hands as my mouth watered at the thought of having him between my lips.

A hand gripped my wrist tight, then set my hand on my own knee as he drew back a little.

"Keep doing that and I'll make good on that promise of inducting you," he growled softly, reaching for me again.

I couldn't help my eyes widening, my breath stuttering a second time. Did that mean— had he—? The mix of triumph and knowledge in his eyes swayed me.

Until his back went rigid, a line of curses spitting from between clenched lips. "Damnit, not my ass." Noah grunted, reaching back to rub himself.

Miss Katherine appeared over his shoulder, grinning as she waved her zap stick.

"**I**'m coming, too." Chrissy planted her feet right between me and the exit to the airport.

Not that I planned on going anywhere but a fishing trip without her any time soon.

The problem was that she wanted to be on that fishing trip.

"We've had hours for that, honey," I said, as much to see the flush rise in her cheeks and her eyes widen with shock as to cover our destination.

"Boys' day out," Queen sang, his arm slung about Chrissy's shoulder as he pivoted her around in a dance and hauled her toward the exit.

Chrissy sent me a plaintitive look over her shoulder, all doe-eyed, but the sparkle beneath betrayed that she enjoyed every moment of it.

After Miss Katherine shocked me for the second time, she provided us both with tiny bags of cookies. Claiming she handed them out to veterans—though I suspected her tame security guard might also be a recipient—she had left us alone, pocketing her cattle prod, and gone to pester the nice air marshall who must have been less than half her age.

"She's got more balls than I'll ever have," I muttered, somewhat in awe.

Joker caught my eye, nudging his feet across my vacated seat.

I waved my okay and settled next to Chrissy, who had done my shirt back up. "Want to watch something?" I murmured into her ear.

She nestled into me with a contented sigh, tilting the screen to share it. I barely watched the art house film she chose, too busy with memorising every curve of her body and how perfectly she fit into me.

Her cry tore me from the memory, my hands already missing the shape of her in them.

"Please, in the name of art," she wailed theatrically as the Tran twins herded her away.

I laughed, hitching my laptop back over my shoulder. Claiming to be a photographer—purely for pleasure—had gotten me through Tongan customs with everything I needed to work out why the boats weren't coming back. Hearts' miniature tool kit that he hoisted over his shoulder provided the rest of our kit for surveillance. We rarely flew commercial, and I was surprised we hadn't lost anything, though we'd packed conservatively, erring on the high side.

This was to be a surveillance mission, nothing more, though I suspected Ace held his cards close to his chest for this one. Usually, he was open with information, and we learned early on together that every bit of data we didn't have could cost us, no matter how much it seemingly might be inane.

I hoped we wouldn't cross that line again. We'd already lost a soldier due to that mishap.

Which brought us back to the fishing trip.

The twins got her as far as the door before Chrissy dug her heels in. Seeming to sense impending separation—though I had already put my number in her phone and texted myself the message—she reversed the roles on the boys in a flash.

Sweet-talking the nearest federal cop, she drew attention to both twins, all smiles and batted eyelashes the guard ate up as he listened. A smile grew on his own face as he called out to one of the locals, a giant of a man, who took both boys off her hands and dragged them to the bar.

Suddenly, I had two very different faces peering back at me with plaintive eyes.

Laughing, I caught up with her at the door.

"Should I wait for them?" I asked, sliding my arm around her waist and pulling her into me, lest the federal cop have ideas that went beyond his pay grade.

"They'll be awhile." Chrissy pressed against my side, her warmth soaking into me.

"What in all the fresh hells are the Trans doing?" Hearts asked, grabbing at the door of the first cab he hailed.

"I told Mafu," she gave the federal cop a little wave that the big man returned, "that they had a bet on how soon they could land some double action. He was happy to oblige."

Hearts' face froze. It wasn't a look I often saw on the big guy.

I shook my head at her.

Joker smiled faintly, hailing his own cab.

"You're mad." I drew her into the backseat of the cab Hearts stopped.

"Can I go on the boat now, please? There's room," she begged prettily.

I kicked Hearts' seat to ease the stab of desire that bolted straight to my dick. "Having a travel blogger on board might help. She has skills." I adjusted the front of my jeans, pulling the door closed.

"Are you really going to leave them there?" she laughed at me.

"Joker'll wait for them if they decide to come back. If not..." I wiggled my eyebrows. It was her turn to flush pink, her mouth forming a tiny 'o'. "Where are you staying?"

Chrissy rattled off an address by heart, adding a few native words into her conversation with the driver.

He shot into a small flow of traffic leaving the airport.

"Wait, this is our hotel." I frowned. *Hotel* was pushing it. The highrise was more a resort than anything else. The driver dropped us at the door, giving Chrissy his card.

"There are a million places you could stay. Why here?" I drove a tiny seed of doubt deep, but the thing kept bouncing back.

Collecting my key was easy; following her to her room after off loading my bags to Hearts wasn't.

Her hand wrapped around mine in the elevator.

I kept waiting for that perfect minute to ask, but every second floor someone hopped onto the elevator or off, and my chance slipped by at the same rate that my control frayed. My palm pressed to my thigh, I missed my sidearm at that moment, but the same message had come from Ace: no weapons.

Zero suspicion that we were anything more than our cover story.

Finally, we reached Chrissy's floor.

She fidgeted with her key card, turning it over between her palms.

"Nervous, honey?" I stroked reassuring fingers along her spine, tugging her into me the way I had the entire trip, but the only energy I felt was the sort that flooded me during an engagement.

The sort of engagement that was filled with lead, not diamonds.

Chrissy shot me a quick look, those gorgeous eyes wide as she flashed her card at the door, and the thing clicked open.

She stepped into the prelit hall of her suite, paused there.

I tugged her bags from her shoulder, letting them drop to the floor. Kicking the door closed behind us, I slid my hands around her arms, pulling her sharply back into me.

She stiffened, failing to hide the gasp that tore from her lips as her back pressed against my front.

Any other time, I would have revelled in the curve of that delicious ass pressing against me, but now was the time for work.

Playing came later.

Maybe.

"Why are you staying in the same place as us, Chrissy? Why were you on the same flight?" I brushed my lips against the side of her neck, inhaling her, wanting her.

Goddam, she smells good.

"I'm doing what?" she leaned back into me, her head tilted back against my shoulder. Luscious curls fell over my hands.

I traced my tongue over her racing pulse.

You're not a good liar, Chrissy.

She moaned softly, stretching in my arms to touch me, but I held her at bay. I needed my head clear for this. And if I turned her around, there was no way I would be thinking with the right one.

"Focus, Chrissy." I nipped where her shoulder creased, eliciting another moan. "After all, you just seemed to be in the right place whenever I turned around."

"What?" She stilled in my grip, her fingers curled around my shoulders.

"You were in the right place in Cambodia. Then you were on my flight. Now, you're staying in my hotel. And your heart is racing."

"*What?*" She jerked around, facing me with slightly wild eyes that narrowed, honing in on me.

Ah, there she is.

The hours wrapped around her had taught me one thing—the girl had a brain on her that could easily rival any of our boys. It was a pity we would never be able to employ her and benefit from that. Fast thinking, and not afraid to take a calculated risk to get what she wanted, she was perfect for the role we each played.

Maybe too perfect.

I tipped her chin back with my knuckle, the only part of me touching her. "Tell me why those things happened."

"You are a first class asshole," she snapped, not tearing her gaze from me. "I should have known that when you shoved me face first in your crotch while I was being shot at, then abandoned me to eleven hours of hell in a police station I thought I might never walk out of again," she seethed, holding up a hand when I opened my mouth. "Oh hell no, Noah, you do *not* get to stop me just because you got a woman who will talk back to you. You know why I'm nervous? Do you?" She poked my chest with a straight finger, pacing toward me until she stood flush against me.

My hands closed around her waist purely by reflex at having her near me. "I am sorry about the police station. That was unavoidable," I said softly.

"That's a shitty apology. That place made Miss Katherine look like a walk down the Vegas strip." She snorted. "Do you know why I'm nervous, Noah King?"

I stared down at her with hard eyes, giving no quarter. I knew this roleplay, and how it would turn out. Not that I was objecting. I just didn't want to wake up with a knife in my back.

Chrissy inhaled, her lips set in a tight line, though her eyes told a different story. "I'm nervous because you dropped your bags with your friend and came back to my room. I didn't offer, Noah. And I don't do this. Ever." She dropped her hand, her energy deflating as quickly as the storm had come on.

I watched her, but her head didn't drop, and her eyes never left mine.

Everything about her was on display and this time I read the nerves, the way she arced up at my assumptions, seeing the duality of her hesitation and need waring deep in her eyes. From the way she tried not to flinch when I moved, though muted desire lit her face.

I'd been wrong.

"Ah, damn, Chrissy." I reached out, widening my arms around her.

The crack of her palm on skin echoed in the short hall.

"Don't you dare. Get out," she snapped, her voice as brittle as my pride.

I rubbed my cheek. "Not the bitch slap I was expecting today."

Chrissy stood still before me, and said nothing.

Using the cover of tending my jaw, I assessed her. Though she didn't back away, I also didn't hold a lot of hope of mending the mess I made. I'd jumped in on her, letting my own paranoia overflow without really scoping out whether she was the threat I expected her to be.

And therein lay the crux of the problem.

I hadn't suspected Chrissy to be batting for another team, I flat out jumped into believing that she was. Despite what she told me about herself during the flight, though none of it had stuck in my thick head.

There was probably little chance of salvaging the situation. The best I could do was to make sure she wasn't left in an emotional mess of my own making.

I swore inwardly at myself as an utter idiot.

Chrissy had warned me she wasn't a hookup girl. But the way she melted against me when I kissed her, the energy inside her that she restrained, that kept her going under pressure drew me to her. That pushed aside my reservations about earning a slap on the other cheek.

I eased closer, watchful of wayward hands or the need to escape me in her eyes, but neither were present.

"I'm sorry, Chrissy." Regret bubbled in my chest, and I pushed it back down. *This isn't about me.* "I didn't think it through. We— damnit, I—" I bit my words off, unable to say anything about my job to her.

Every damn time I get close to someone.

Which, for the last few years, hadn't been very often. But then, we'd all know what we were when we signed up for Z Unit. The type of glorified cannon fodder that was left to rot in an overseas jail with no record, if we weren't shot on the spot.

There was no room in my life, in *any* of our lives, for a permanent relationship.

It was why the Tran boys acted out.

It was why Joker always had his resting fuck off face at the ready.

It was why Hearts hadn't objected to being part of a family for the brief flight.

Permanence wasn't meant for men like us.

"It's okay." She wrapped warm fingers around my hand, tracing over the grazed knuckles.

I glanced at her in surprise. "No, honey. It's far from okay. I should go."

Chrissy planted both hands on my chest. "You were doing your job, and I'm guessing you'd be pretty shitty at it if you didn't watch out for things like that." One hand raised to touch my cheek, tracing the invisible mark there.

I caught her hand. "You're too forgiving."

Chrissy laughed. "That's not something I think I've ever heard before."

"It's true." I turned into her palm, catching her wrist to kiss her fingertips. "How forgiven am I?"

Her lips pursed, but her eyes resumed their sparkle above them. "You might have to keep working on that. And lose the hideous shirt." She laughed.

"Done."

The shirt was off in a second. I stood still, letting her see the collection of scars that marred my side.

Her eyes tracked from my shoulders, over my chest and lingered where a mess of flesh was highlighted by a pair of tiny, puckered dots below my ribs.

"You go shot. Twice," Chrissy drew her fingers over the mess. "Can you feel that?" When she looked up at me, the only thing that filled her eyes was compassion, not the disgust I was so used to. A pretty face didn't cover the ruined man I had become.

"A bit." I shrugged, forcing myself to hold still. Waited for the disgust that was sure to come to settle in.

Chrissy's fingers travelled a little lower, sliding across my abs in a feather touch.

"And that?" she asked, her voice soft.

"Yeah," I managed, squeezing my hands into fists, letting my nails bite into my palms as her hand skated lower, tracing along the top of my jeans.

I caught her wrist, pulling her slowly into me, giving her time to push me away.

Her soft gasp hardened me instantly, her rainforest scent swirled around me until she was everything.

Chrissy's curls tumbled over my hands as I curved them around her back. Everything about her was light and small. Fragile, but strong. I'd known it since I had her head in my lap in Cambodia.

Her heart pounded fast against my chest as she tilted her head back, heavy lidded eyes staring into mine.

The fingers I wound into her hair tightened, tugging a little. Chrissy arched into me, her body pressed flush against mine as she pushed up onto her toes with a soft moan that removed the last, pathetic remnant of resistance in me.

My mouth crashed down over hers. I swept my tongue between her lips, tasting her. Our tongues twiled inside her mouth, stroking in a heady dance that went straight to my dick. I wound my arms around her tight, clinging to the few minutes, an hour if I was lucky, that I would be able to immerse myself in her.

Every breath drew a soft moan from her lips until she stole my air.

I walked her backward until my knuckles hit the wall, cushioning her head as I pressed my weight into her against it.

My kisses became harder, releasing the strain of the last few hours, touching her when all I wanted was to be inside her, to have her wrapped around me.

Untangling my fingers gently from her hair, I slid my hands down to her hips, grazing my fingertips over her ass. She wiggled sweetly, rubbing that body that I'd needed since I'd first seen her against me.

Gripping her tight, I lifted her onto my hips, pressing her back against the wall.

Her lips parted, a soft cry tearing from between them.

"King," she whimpered, wrapping her arms around my neck for leverage to rub herself against me, seeking friction for her own pleasure. The heat emanating from her body contacted mine, and it was hot as hell.

"Fuck," I swore. I wasn't going to last long if she kept doing that.

The material of her shirt was soft and stretchy, sliding over her head with ease. I pulled her higher up the wall, trapping her there with my body. A flick of the back on her bra with one hand released the clasp and I pulled it free.

"Well practiced," she muttered.

"Are you grumpy, girl?" I laughed, grazing beneath her breasts with my thumbs. That earned me another gasp. "Honestly?" Her nipples already pebbled, I pinched and tugged at them, rolling them between my fingers.

"No," she gasped, her sweet little sigh doing mad things to my brain as she writhed beneath my touch.

When I claimed her mouth again, I'd already mapped out a vague path to the bedroom through a glimpse down the hall.

Chrissy clung to me, her arms wrapped around my shoulders, her lips making gentle patterns on my neck. Her tongue stroked my skin, reminding me of her mouth on my cock through my jeans, her head moving over me as I held her there.

My breath came short and my strides lengthened.

Three doorways and half a hall later, we tumbled into the bedroom.

We never made it to the bed.

CHAPTER SEVEN

CHRISSY

Noah's mouth was still on mine when my back hit the soft carpet. His arms cushioned the fall, rolling me with him onto his back so I straddled him.

"Classy." I smirked, knowing my hair was an absolute wild nest that tumbled over both of us.

He stretched out beneath me, golden and perfect.

My gaze lit on the mutilated section of skin around his ribs that covered down to his hip. Someone else might object to it. All that scarring told me was that the man beneath me had the courage not only to do something that might get him injured like he had, but also to display it. Baring everything to someone who could reject him took a different kind of bravery, as shallow a thing as that might be. Or not.

I could appreciate that sort of courage in a man. I didn't care about the shallow bit, but I was afraid I'd already offered my heart to Noah, and I didn't know what he would do with it. Tugging the button of his jeans free, I undulated my hips against him in a slow rhythm.

His chest rose and fell, slow and calm.

Not the man who almost lost control in the entrance of my suite.

Noah's answering smile to my smirk was all cat-got-the-cream. He traced along my ribs with light fingertips, brushing gently across the tops of my breasts, then down to the nipples, playing with them.

I had never met a man skilled in pinching a nipple, had thought they were a dime-store book fallacy. But Noah King gave me hope.

"Wait, just for a second." I covered his hands with mine.

He paused and quirked an eyebrow. "You want me to stop?"

"Yes. I need to breathe. And," I leaned back onto his shins, wiggling free of my jeans, "I need to get these off."

"Not a bad plan." Noah's gaze raked over me, his lips curling with appreciation. Desire swirled in his sapphire dark gaze.

I froze, the deer in the headlights who knows the oncoming impact is going to rewrite every part of her. Kicking my shoes and jeans off, I crawled back along his legs.

Feeling the weight of his gaze on me, I tugged his jeans down over his hips. His boxers slid down easily, the memory of the shape of him against my lips a dream until now.

He fit perfectly in my hand. I stroked him gently, waiting for his breath to quicken before I dipped my head and finally tasted him.

Denim and sweat.

Everything I remembered about him flooded back. I explored with my tongue, settling onto my knees. This time, when his hand tangled into my hair and he pushed me down onto him, a rush of pleasure replaced the fear and adrenaline of our first encounter. The need to know every inch of him—and there were plenty of those to be had—was finally satisfied.

Noah groaned, tugging me the length of his body.

"I wasn't finished," I protested.

"I nearly was." He swept hair away from my face, curling his hand around the back of my neck in a familiar motion. His fingers turned circles there that sent shivers to my toes, "and I need to give you more than that."

He rolled us again, pinning me beneath him on the carpet with his substantial body weight, muscles straining beneath his tanned skin as he braced himself on one arm. The other dug in his discarded jeans, extracting a tiny packet he tore open with his teeth.

I tugged the rubber gently from the packet, reaching between us to rub my hands the length of him. But I wasn't the only one exploring.

Noah trailed his fingers along my stomach to dip gently between my thighs, tracing the soft mound of flesh there. He circled around the peak of every nerve ending, dipping inside me as I managed to get the tip of the condom sorted, attempting to roll it the length of him.

Noah slid two fingers inside me, filling me.

I arched beneath him, biting back a moan, the condom finally rolling down properly.

Bonus points for multi-tasking, Chrissy.

His eyes caught mine and held. Their brilliant, deep blue pierced straight through me as his fingers moved slowly inside me. My hips moved with him until he curled his fingers to hit a sensitive spot.

My body convulsed. I gripped his shoulder tight, the pleasure he gave sweeping over me.

Noah's arm wrapped around my back, holding me up against him as his fingers slid gently from me, leaving me empty.

I made a pathetic noise of protest, the rumble in his chest doing nothing to help my situation.

"I promise, honey. It's worth waiting."

That same promise glowed in his eyes as he dipped his head to kiss me, his tongue plundering and dancing against mine until my head swam with the mixed touches.

Demanding, then sweet; claiming, then gentle.

The man was a hundred different things at once, and everything to me.

His cock pressed against my entrance. My breath caught, I leaned up to kiss him, wiggling my hips.

Noah's hand came down on my stomach. "Easy, honey. Let's take this slow."

"I didn't think you were a slow type of guy," I huffed against his lips.

"I'm not," he agreed, sliding inside me smoothly until our bodies joined completely.

A cry caught in my throat, I pressed my lips to his shoulder. "King," I whispered.

His hands wrapped around into my hair, cupping my head so I had to look up at him. "Are you okay?" he asked, kissing me gently. "Am I hurting you?"

I nodded, then shook my head. "Yes, okay. No, not hurting," I reassured him, my breaths short and shallow. "It's just a lot of everything at once."

"Let me fix that," he murmured, moving slowly against me.

My body adjusted to the loss of him within me before he just as slowly filled me again. Every nerve ending screamed to keep him buried inside me, pleasure overriding everything else.

"This is not fixing it," I gasped, though I wasn't protesting.

"No," Noah smiled, kissing me deeply, "it's blocking everything else out."

He glided over me, setting a rhythm of his own. I moved my body to match his pace, wrapping my calves behind his thighs to draw him closer.

Noah braced one forearm over my head, his other wrapped tight around me, lifting me off the floor as his rhythm grew faster, harder. Something let loose in him, tearing free.

And for the second time, the pleasure he gave me obliterated everything else. I cried my release, a wanton sound that matched my own greedy movements, craving more of him even as he satisfied me.

Noah held my gaze, his sapphire eyes darkening to a tempest in the sea. A primal growl built in his chest, his movements becoming erratic until his pleasure roared over me, taking me with him a second time.

"Your chest is incredibly comfortable," I murmured.

Every limb anchored me into him. My breaths matched his heartbeat, the slow, steady rhythm that was all Noah King.

"So are you." Noah's fingers tangled in my hair, the circles that started on my neck running across my shoulders and along my back in a leisurely path. "So, sorry about this."

His hands slid around me, shifting us both as he rose, still leaning back and deposited me onto a soft, if somewhat cold, surface.

I buried my face into the quilt with a groan, my hair tumbling around my shoulders to cover me in a curtain that did nothing to hide me.

"Damnit, Noah," I muttered into the thick, soft cotton.

He was back in a moment, rolling me gently onto my back, a warm washcloth in his hand. Noah tidied both of us up, his gentle touch evoking tiny aftershocks I knew he saw.

His body slid beneath mine again, pulling me over him like a blanket.

"Not overwhelming anymore?" he asked, resuming the patterns he trailed along my back.

"Not any more." I snuggled against him. "I'm just shattered."

"They say exercise is good for anxiety."

"Is that what they say?" I yawned, barely getting my hand up to cover my mouth.

"Yeah." Noah stretched up, sliding his hand beneath his head. The lines on his carved face softened, tension released to free him of the restraints he seemed to constantly carry.

"You look satisfied." I propped my chin on his chest, studying him, but nothing changed about him in the last few minutes.

"I am." Endless blue eyes returned my assessment. Long, lean muscles shaped the hard surface of him, but the warmth that seemed to emanate from his chest drew me down. "You too tired for a boat trip?" he murmured, shifting so my legs tangled around his, until I lost where I ended and he started.

"I forgot about the boat." I closed my eyes, pressing into his chest. Had that really only been an hour or two ago? It felt like an age since we got off the plane.

"Rest, honey. We'll sort everything in a bit."

The beat of his heart against my cheek obliterated the world around us, his voice fading with it until there was only the warmth and safety his arms around me offered.

"Are you ready to help me out?" Noah asked some indeterminable time later, sliding his arm around my waist to draw me into his chest. His kiss was languid and deep and brought heat rushing to every surface.

"What am I doing?" I asked in a dozy voice, staring up at him with my head tilted back. I could barely focus when he kissed me.

"Fuck, girl." Noah leaned down to kiss me again, all the gentleness and sweet caresses traded in for something far more demanding, something possessive.

I rose to my knees with a gasp as he drew me up and broke the kiss with a slap on my ass. "Ow," I murmured, though I was certain my cheeks were tinted pink.

"We're never going to get anywhere if you keep looking that cute."

"I'm cute?"

"As a button." He kissed me again and pushed up off the bed. "Do you need food?"

"I—" I covered my stomach as it rumbled on cue. "Maybe lunch?" I murmured, slightly horrified that we spent so much energy in doing the horizontal folk dance that I was ravenous.

"Let's do it. I want to plan out the day and get this job done. It leaves me more time for you," Noah murmured, sliding his arms around my waist to pull me into him.

"I thought you said no more of this?" I asked, nipping his bottom lip, lightening with a grin.

"Just making sure I'm in character. You don't get embarrassed by PDAs, do you?" His eyes sparkled. A flicker of heat burned in the depths in his arctic blue eyes that read as a promise directed right at me.

Damn it, he had all the makings of an exhibitionist.

The problem was that I *was* uncomfortable with any display of affection in public. Just me, not anyone else. Kissing Noah on the plane had been completely out of character, as had the romantic whirlwind that had ended up with us in my bedroom. These things didn't happen to a travel blogger. The romance myth was just that, and the dream never came true.

Well, maybe once.

"A tiny bit," I hedged, letting a question slide into my gaze. "I'm not into voyeurism or anything."

Noah stared down at me. The ice blue embers in his eyes burned darker. "Pity," he murmured, sweeping his lips over my cheek, along my throat. "Kissing will do, but you'll have to make it look real."

"I'll have to make it look real, Mister King?" I asked, my eyebrows raised. "I'm having a shower. Then food. Then go and kiss me in public all you want for your investigation thing."

"Yes, ma'am," he laughed at me, swatting at me again.

I shrieked and tumbled off the bed, landing in a pile of sheets and quilts on the floor. Noah knelt to lift me up to him, but the moment his hands slid around my waist, the distraction became a real one.

We didn't make it down to lunch for some time.

Sea spray stung my face in tiny drops. Noah had paid out a small fortune for an overpriced speed boat for hire that could have been called a small yacht. Rather than wait for his friends who hadn't yet emerged from their rooms or answered his calls, except for a single message that had him frowning, he tugged me out onto the dock, tickling me and laughing. It belatedly occured to me that we must look like any couple on their honeymoon, or a romantic getaway, and wondered how much of his enjoyment was real, and how much was an act.

He draped his arm across my shoulders as he drove, squeezing gently. I knew I still had the *I've just been fucked* glow. I'd met him in brief encounters, and spent more time in bed with him, skin-to-skin, than anything else. We might be strangers to each other, but to everyone else in the world, we were a loved up couple on holiday at a tropical island.

"What are we looking for?" I shifted in my leather covered seat, running my fingertips over the polished wood of the boat. "Is there someone you're targeting?"

Noah sent me a sideways glance, the corners of his lips turned up. His gaze did odd things to my stomach. I distracted myself with a study of him, and that turned out to be a terrible idea. Dressed in a white button down casual shirt and camel coloured pants, he was the epitome of a beach model. The thin shirt showed the silhouette of his ripped and hardened musculature which I was beginning to know well. Heat rushed to my cheeks beneath his knowing gaze.

"Hey, what was that?" He turned his attention from the ocean to draw me into a long kiss. When he drew back, my cheeks weren't the only things that were red.

"That was me paddling totally out of my depths, and feeling very small," I said, leaning back against his shoulder.

Noah's arm tightened around me, a hint of the possessiveness I thought I saw in him rushing back to me. I snuggled deeper.

"Good girl," he murmured, his lips close enough to my ear to be heard over the constant whine of the engine.

I shivered, and his arm tightened. This—whatever *this* was—had happened so fast that I could barely keep up with him. It felt less like a three encounter fling and more like something that could last longer. But that wasn't possible with whatever his job was. It was clear his team was military, or paramilitary, and for all the jokes and fun, I knew from my experience that a killer, when need called upon it, resided in every single one of them.

So why did I feel safe in Noah's arms? I should have been running for the hills, not playing holiday makers and renting a boat. Which drew me back before I rambled on in my head and planned a beach elopement.

Oh, hell no.

I blinked and shoved that one as far away from me as possible.

"There's nothing out here but ocean, Noah. There's nothing on the maps." I pressed my palm to the plethora of touristy maps he encouraged me to pick up at reception. I'd been as happy as a clam by the time we left reception. "There's nothing out here."

"What I'm looking for won't be on a map." Noah scanned the dark blue line of the horizon with a fixed stare. "I'll know it when I see it."

Well that cleared things up, thanks very much. I changed tack.

"What do you do?"

"What do I do?" He sent me an amused look, then turned his attention back to the water.

I stared around us, but the water was empty. There weren't even any other holiday goers around. Not a boat, a whale watching cruise, a deep sea fishing charter. No small plane flights or gliders. Nothing. Just us. It was...peaceful.

I leaned back, relaxing for the first time since he put me into the boat. I decided to poke the bear.

"Yes, Mister Military. What do you do? In your...group."

"Am I in a band? Does that make you my groupie?" His eyes sparkled at me, and I knew I was okay to keep asking questions.

"No!" I laughed, squeezing his side gently, tracing my fingers over his ribs. "What do you do? Like that day in—"

I never got to finish my sentence.

Noah's mouth slammed down over mine, stealing my breath and my words with his demands. His tongue drove deep between my lips as his hand cupped the back of my head, pulling me up into him. When he broke the kiss, my lips were tender and I had no breath left at all.

Noah brushed his mouth over mine in an apology, though his eyes held a warning as he stroked my cheek, drawing me into him. "Damn, girl. I should have warned you there was no chance of me not getting in your pants out here."

I smothered a squeak in his shirt, pressing my lips to the material in a kiss. "You did warn me," I agreed, emboldened by his kiss, the need of it. *Please tell me that wasn't all playacting and he meant that kiss.* On the other hand, if he meant everything he had put into it, then I was in deep trouble.

Tracing my hands down his chest, I stroked over his washboard abs, tracing along the line of his belt.

"I thought you said you weren't into voyeurism?" he asked lightly, but his humour barely covered the tension in his voice, its edge heavy with desire as I stroked my hand over his cock through his pants.

He caught my wrist in a light but firm grip, and I looked up in surprise when he gave the tiniest shake of his head.

"I thought you would—"

His mouth landed on mine again, stealing my words a second time. His kiss was gentler than before, back to the languid, thigh-parting kisses of the bedroom. I moaned softly when he brushed his thumb beneath my breast, catching the swell of sensitive flesh there.

"Take it slow, Chrissy," he murmured against my mouth. "I'll give you plenty to talk about later."

"Mmhmm," I murmured, sinking back into him.

"Fuck." Noah drew back from me, his gaze returning to the water.

I focused on the water for a moment, but saw nothing. A few small dots and a slightly bigger one appeared on the horizon.

I squinted. "What is it? And how the hell could you see that before me?" There was nothing wrong with my eyes. But apparently his were exceptional.

"Practice," he said, his voice tense, as he pulled me closer into his side, working at the buttons of my dress with one hand. He kissed me again, ruffling my hair so that even with the speed we travelled at, it appeared more than boat-mussed. Noah nipped my bottom lip.

I squealed as he looked down at his handiwork and gave me a smile that was filled with promise I had no doubt he would claim later.

"Are you done?" I demanded, but the effect was lost when I drifted against him, caught in the current of him that dragged me along.

"With you? Never. But now you look the part." His gaze swept over me appreciatively.

"What, and you don't need to be all rumpled and ruffled and..." I resembled a guppie as I struggled for words, my brain refusing to function in the wake of his kisses.

"Just fucked?" Noah suggested lightly, squeezing my shoulder. He turned back to the water and swerved the boat for zero reason I could see. "Here we go."

I focused on the three small dots that formed into jet skis with riders in black as we drew nearer to them in a collision course. A large pleasure cruiser that must have been several millions of dollars worth of fibreglass cruised behind them.

Noah swore again, and after a long moment of study to see what he saw, I echoed his sentiment.

Every black-clothed rider carried a weapon, the same sort that I had become so intimately familiar with in Cambodia.

"Fuck."

Noah nodded and set us in an intercept course.

CHAPTER EIGHT

KING

So much for a day out on the water doing surveillance. Ace was going to hand me my ass for bringing a civilian out with me on the job.

Suddenly, Joker's earlier message about missing local fisherman and rumours of boats not coming back got a whole lot more real.

"Is there a reason we're not turning around and running like hell?" Chrissy asked, fear lacing her voice.

I squeezed her shoulder harder. The truth was that a rather enormous part of me did want to turn around and run like hell. This wasn't the place for her to be, and if she got hurt because of my risks and stupidity, it would kill me.

Not even a single day with her and I was already attached to the girl at my side. And in my line of work, that couldn't be allowed to happen.

"If I turn around now, I could lose them. They aren't going to stay in one spot and wait for me to come back with my friends, honey."

And if we ran too efficiently, then they would give chase and without my firearms to protect us, and it would be game over.

Chrissy nibbled her lip and nodded, though I doubted my bullshit excuse convinced her.

The jetskis split to circle either side of us, surrounding us in a every tightening ring of sea spray and intimidation.

I slapped a goofy grin on my face, leaning back to lightly brush my fingers over Chrissy's breast. She froze and made me look like a wealthy white boy chump.

Perfect.

"Keep that up and we're good," I murmured, waving to our aggressive crowd with my free hand. I slowed the engine and left it to idle.

Chrissy pressed her knee against mine.

I gave her hand a squeeze as one rider pulled up beside us.

"Hi." I smiled genially at the three jet skis as though they weren't circling us like sharks, rose out of my seat with a stumble, and managed to stub my toe for real. Keeping that off my face became a new struggle. "Out for a drive with the lady. Hope we're not crossing an international line." I laughed too loudly, keeping the gumby look plastered on my face, and I saw the moment the man next to me bought my act.

He jerked his chin, and the two men behind us peeled away in a shower of recycled sea water.

Chrissy squawked on cue. Suppressing a grin, I filed the moment away to thank her for the response later.

"Stay back near the island. There are rips out here that will drag you under, and you'll never get to finish your holiday." The man stared at me, and I held his gaze, nodding like a bobblehead toy on a car dash, my cheeks aching with my fake humour.

Let me get my rifle and we will see who gets to finish their fucking holiday.

But I didn't have the tool with me that had earned me my coveted Crossed Rifles badge, and only my smart mouth to combat the man next to me.

"Yeah, sure, of course! What a nice man." I half-turned to Chrissy as I spoke, and prayed I didn't get shot in the back. "Wasn't there something on at the resort later tonight? A bingo hall?"

Chrissy giggled at me with a vacant expression. Her teeth clenched between her lips, her smile strained at the corners.

"Fuck me," the man muttered. "Go home. Don't come back out here." He revved the jet ski, following his men back to the yacht that motored quietly across the horizon in a single-ship blockade.

Chrissy wound her fingers through mine, but I waited until the jet ski was a speck in the distance before I turned the speedboat around. There was no point in risking turning my back on a man like that twice.

He had shown his face, been open about it, which meant he either had a death wish, or he believed he was untouchable.

That last gave me pause. In my line of work, it wasn't something I saw often, but hell, I was up for the challenge.

Flicking my phone open, I took note of our position and saved it as we pulled away. I set the throttle at full speed. There was a good chance the jet skis could follow us for a distance, but they didn't have the fuel tank of the rental boat, and would have to turn back to the yacht before we reached the relative safety of the shore.

I tapped away at the screen of my phone as I pulled out in a wide, wobbly arc to help cement the impression I was an idiot, though inside, I seethed. I was keen to ensure the unit knew the situation before they walked headlong into something they didn't expect.

But then I was also pissed with myself that I brought Chrissy along into what could have been a fatal incident. There was nothing that could have stopped those men from killing us both and sinking the boat, or let it float to be found in a few days by a local fisherman, or my boss.

He let us swan away, like he owned the fucking ocean.

Out here, maybe he did.

"It's okay," Chrissy murmured, squeezing my hand. She slid across the console, planting her ass over it in what had to be a hugely uncomfortable position, and kissed my cheek.

I wound my fingers through her hair to massage her neck, earning a little mewl that went straight to my cock despite the situation.

"I'm sorry I put you in danger like that," I said into her hair, and half hoped that she couldn't hear me.

"You mean we were in danger?" She tilted her head back to look up at me with a vacant expression, her stare fixed at a point several degrees off the end of my nose.

"Hell, don't do that. You've lowered the IQ of the room."

"Boat."

"Good to see you have your brains back." I kissed her upturned lips, ignoring the arousal that zinged through me.

"Mmhmm." Her fingers trailed down the front of my shirt, brushing over the already hard ridge of my cock through my pants, her lips turned up in a cheeky smile.

Two can play at that game, girl.

I grabbed her hand. "Pretty little hussy. Didn't you get enough cock earlier, honey?" I sent her a wicked smile of my own, loading every fantasy I wanted to play out with her into it.

"Oh," she murmured, her eyes widening.

I kissed her, hard and quick, yanking her hand from me. "Wait. I actually need to concentrate for this next bit." I smiled again, but some of the humour drained from me to be replaced with something darker.

I played the chump in front of a man who was clearly my enemy, but for risking Chrissy in what was clearly not my territory, I was the biggest idiot for it. And my ego had taken a little bruising.

The trip back seemed a lot shorter than our relaxed trip out earlier. I gripped Chrissy's hand tight in mine, though I urged her to slide into her seat. Regardless of the situation, I was unwilling to let her go, though it was probably the first thing I should have done when we reached the pier.

Joker stood on the dock, his arms folded across his chest.

"Subtle," I called, tossing him the mooring rope. "Really fucking subtle. Not like it's your job to blend in."

"He's always like this." Joker rolled his eyes as he addressed Chrissy and ignored me.

"I can tell," she said lightly, though I got the impression she was fairly pissed at my rejection earlier.

I swore softly under my breath as Joker helped her onto the pier. "I need to—"

"It's not a problem," she cut me off with a too-bright smile. "I need material for my blog. Might book into the spa and do some reviews. You boys have a lot to talk about." She flounced along the wooden boards that creaked beneath her rubber sandals.

Joker whistled softly. "The fuck did you do, man?"

"Put her in a position where I couldn't have defended her because I was too loved up and wasn't fucking thinking straight," I ground out. "And I rejected her advances because I was trying to think my way through what we needed to do, and she was a distraction."

"Is that all?" Joker raised an eyebrow, his British accent thickening as he drew the words out. "Reckon it's that last one that sank you."

"Yeah." I scrubbed a hand over my face. "I fucked that up. And I'll make it up to her. C'mon. I'll fill you in at the same time as everyone else."

"More rejection?" Joker clutched at his chest in a pantomime of death. "I'm mortally wounded."

"You bloody well will be if you don't move. We need to fix this." I shoved past his tall frame, striding the length of the pier in the hopes of catching Chrissy, but by the time I reached the hotel foyer, she had disappeared.

"Do you want to check your room?" Joker asked, dangling the temptation he knew I wanted to take.

I didn't correct him that I'd screwed her on the floor of her room, not mine, because it had nothing to do with him.

"Job comes first." I smiled at the receptionist who sat behind the front desk of the building, but she watched me with a wary gaze. I wondered what Chrissy said to her.

"Not Mister Popular anymore, are you?" Joker murmured as I hit the call button for the elevator bank.

I grunted my response and attempted to ignore him until we reached the floor we had taken rooms on, most near each other.

"This one is Hearts'?" I raised my fist over the door to the room I thought was the correct one and hesitated.

Joker nodded. "I'm down there and the Trans are further along."

"Wanna go get them? I think we need everyone, maybe set up a call with Ace."

"That bad? Why the fuck were we dawdling?"

I ran my gaze over him insolently. "We aren't all fucking giraffes. Get the twins."

"Oh, yes, sir." Joker saluted with a serious face that I wanted to punch.

Ignoring his antics, I knocked on the door.

A muffled yell echoed behind it, and a few moments later, the door opened.

Hearts' bulk filled the doorway. "Bored already?" he asked, making way for me to sidle past him, but there wasn't really enough room.

I gave him a look, and headed into the sitting room. The space was filled with computers and medical equipment in a mess that made mine look petty.

"What the hell are you doing?" I asked, stepping around cables that hung from a fake potted palm.

"Surveillance," he pointed to the computers. "Inventory and supplies."

"You really are a one man army, Hearts."

"One part of a well-oiled machine." He perched on his heels, tapping at keyboards on the floor.

"Yeah? Keep your baby oil obsession between you and Ace. I'm not into your slimy shit."

Hearts shrugged, his familiar good natured banter easing the tension that gripped me.

I needed to speak to Chrissy and smooth things over, but by the sound of things, she had her own set of distractions. If I got the job done, then I could spend all the time she needed for me to convince her not to hold a grudge.

The fantasy of her on her back in my bed with her legs in the air while I knelt between them making my apologies with my tongue swept through my mind, leaving me painfully hard and distracted yet again.

This was becoming a bad damn habit. A break in attention could be fatal in my line of work. It nearly had been earlier in the day. My tension returned. I clenched my fists at my sides, inhaling slowly, and let it all out.

Joker strode through down the corridor with a sour look on his face.

Hearts looked up at him from his position on the floor with a frown. "The fuck did you get into my room, Brit?"

Joker flicked his wrist, displaying a full spread of door keycards.

I counted quietly and turned away, a smile spreading over my face that I wasn't ready for him to see, though I checked my pocket to be sure.

"Don't bother. These are spares. The lovely lady on reception provided them at check in, seeing as I'm your boss for this trip." He slipped one of the six into my palm.

I stared at the card with Chrissy's name written across the top and nodded my thanks. My distraction has been so complete, I hadn't noticed him do it when we had arrived at the hotel. From the look on Hearts' face, neither had he.

Already missing Chrissy near me, and after this morning I was glad to have a way to get to her at all times. It mightn't be all above board, but neither were we.

Joker's words clicked into place in my head. "Wait, boss?"

"You are fucking not." Queen strolled into the room, slipping around Joker to deposit an armful of laundry in the middle of the room on top of everything. "Ours broke. Please?" He batted false eyelashes at Hearts.

The big man nodded as the second Tran twin skirted around Joker on his other side. "Out the back. But you hang it out yourself."

"Oh, no, that's my job." Knave winked. He collected the bundle his twin had dropped and disappeared down another hallway that ostensibly led to a laundry.

"Whatever works." Queen shrugged.

"What's happened?" Hearts asked. "I didn't know we had any reconnaissance planned yet."

"We didn't." Joker wiggled his fingers at me. "He fucked up."

"Do you have to look so damn delighted about it?" I grumbled, running a hand through my hair. The point stung, because Joker was right. I had gone off the reservation a little.

"Always. Covers my own ass for when I do it." Joker shrugged, sending me a quick grin.

"Fair 'nuff." I planted my ass on the edge of the coffee table, waiting until the room quieted. "I took a little boat ride with Chrissy."

"Ohhh, she has a name," Queen cooed.

"And we ended up out on the edge of something that could have gotten both of us killed. I sent you the coordinates." I wallowed in my guilt for a minute, let it cover the need to banter it out with Queen.

Hearts nodded, watching me. The big man's assessing gaze was worse than Ace ripping me a new one.

"We were stopped by a group of men on jet skis." I outlined our encounter, cursing myself as an utter idiot. Chrissy seemed like a fun prop when we were on land, but once we were away from everyone that belief had dwindled fast."

"What was the name of the boat?"

"The *Matriarch*." I described the yacht to him as Hearts tapped at his keyboard. I hand't spoken to Chrissy about it after realising what a shock it had been to her that I was able to see so far. Years of sniper training and being blessed with damn good eyesight honed a few skills. But there was no point in scaring her with those just yet.

"Not registered."

"Is that a surprise?"

"Probably not," he murmured, still tapping. A view of the ocean around the island filled his screen.

"Is that live?" I leaned past him.

"Thirty minute delay. I hacked into a few local satellites." Hearts studied the screen dragging the blank water over the screen. There wasn't a fishing boat in sight. "We need to get out there," Hearts murmured.

"A second time? I doubt they will be as friendly. And it's hard to sneak up on something that's floating in the middle of nowhere with three hundred and sixty degrees of vision." I shrugged. "Have we got a drone?"

It was a brilliant strategy, in hindsight. We just needed to know what they were doing and how they were doing it.

"We have the Wasp." Hearts pointed to a row of tech that was neatly lined up and partly obscured by cables.

Joker muttered something about Beirut as he picked his way through the mess, and collected it. "What's the range on that, and how far out were you?" he asked.

"Twenty nautical miles," I said.

"Fifteen minutes and not that far," Hearts replied with a grimace.

Not having our usual assortment of tech and goodies was crippling to a degree, but that's what we got for flying commercial and undercover. No toys.

"Damn. Okay, we put someone out in a boat and send it out."

I opened my mouth to say it wasn't a good idea, but another thought popped into my head. "Fishing charter?"

It had been the original plan, but I'd well and truly blown our chance on that first shot at surveillance now. The *Matriarch's* men were unlikely to be friendly the second time.

Hearts considered for a long moment. I could almost see the cogs turning over in his head. "Alright. I can acquire a boat. Do we risk a local as the driver?"

"What about one of the fishermen you spoke to?" I asked Joker. "They might be able to point out where the issues have been. There's likely a section of water they won't fish now, and it'll become a superstition if this keeps up." I mulled it over. "We didn't see a single other boat or tourist attraction out on the water."

Maybe that was exactly what the antagonistic group wanted. But what in the hell were they doing out there? The whole situation started to feel like a nineteen sixties spy film, and I grew more uncomfortable with the not knowing factor with every minute.

Hearts was talking, and I shook my head to clear it, catching Joker's warning glance.

"...we'll go with the fishing charter plan. I'll acquire what we need, unless you have a contact?" He glanced up at Joker from his position on the floor.

Joker nodded. "Yeah, I got it."

"Good. We play out on the water, see what we can find out. King, you're on the top of the building. It's the only high point with greater clarity on this side of the island."

"What?" I jerked back like I'd been strung. "I'm grounded?"

"If you want to see it that way." Joker smirked.

I itched to bitch-slap the smarmy little smile right off his face.

"I got you toys." Hearts studied me, his gaze filled with understanding. "We need support. Plus, you've got your scope."

I pressed my lips into a hard line. "A scope is meant to make me feel better?"

Hearts huffed. "And this." He reached backward to tug a camel blanket off an old Mauser Gewher 98 rifle Lee-Enfield that looked like it had last been fired in nineteen forty-two. Two tattered packs of ammunition and a cleaning kit sat next to it.

A grin split my face. "Holy shit. Where did you dig up that fossil?" I slipped off the coffee table, examining the rifle. "It's an antique."

"It was the best I could find you." Hearts grinned at my enthusiasm as I began to dismantle the thing.

It might look old, but it was well loved and oiled. He nudged a small stack of ammo my way. I ran my fingers over the barrel. There was plenty of room to add my scope on top. I'd need to fit it, though.

"Thanks. Do you have the tool box?" Nothing ominous, the tool box was filled with miniature tools that gave us a quick and easy fix when we had to rig something up, and had held most of the surveillance kit that currently covered Hearts' living area floor.

"Over there." Hearts pointed. "Alright, let's get this done before we lose these suckers. King, you're on support. Go relax for a bit, don't get caught up in anything. We'll need your eyes."

If I could see that far.

In reality, I'd be as likely to see a seagull and be of little use to them. I gritted my teeth.

"Fine," I said softly, my mind already churning. If I could make sure Chrissy wasn't running off and we could talk after the mission was done, then I'd have clear reign to support the unit as needed.

"Focus, dickhead." Joker slapped the back of my head.

I glared at him, though I knew I probably earned it. That chafed more.

"I'm right here," I ground out, my calm of a moment before dissipating.

"And that's where you stay," Joker held my gaze. "Sit."

I flipped him the bird.

"Right. Let's get it done. See you on the dock in twenty." Hearts effectively shooed us out of his room.

"I need to wear something nautical." Queen mused as we filed into the hallway above.

"Can nautical be tactical?" Knave asked.

"We will make it work." Linking his arm though his brother's, Queen skipped down the hall in the direction of the room.

I turned in the direction of my room, clutching the old rifle wrapped in the camel hair blanket, the tool box dangling from my fingers. A hand on my shoulder gave me pause. I didn't look back at Joker, but I did stop.

"Are you going to do what you're told, Noah?" he asked in a soft voice that disguised his accent.

"Don't I always?" I asked with a sigh.

Laughter broke the silence in the corridor behind me. "Fuck no. But it's in all our best interests."

"Fine. I'll support you." I just didn't say *how*.

"Good boy." He ruffled my hair, dodging around me, and was out of my reach before my reflexes kicked in.

I bared my teeth at his back and went to find Chrissy.

My legs were restless with the need to run, the energy I usually pushed through pent up already. Anything fun would have to wait until after the mission. I put power into my stride, burning out a little of the flickering muscles that were desperate for exercise post flight. The boat trip might have used up some energy in anxiety, but there was plenty left to burn.

Pity I didn't have time to find a shooting range and fire off a few rounds. Using an unknown weapon for what was likely to be impossible at best was the fastest way to be labeled as unreliable, but in this instance, I had no other choice.

I checked my room, knowing she would be there, and put the scope together with the rifle and scope rings, making a note to return the tool box to Hearts after we were done.

Once I was satisfied, I stowed it beneath my baggage, and hung the *do not disturb* tag on the door handle on my way out.

I needed to find Chrissy, and I had four minutes before Hearts would expect me to be on the roof.

She wasn't in her room. I used the spare card Joker slipped me to open her door. I did knock first, but I was on the clock and I needed to see her. Swearing louder with each step, I took the stairs at a sprint to the spa rooms, but they were empty. The resort dietician's office was set up next to that, and I checked it too, but no one had seen Chrissy.

Tearing back to my room, I bundled everything into my arms, knowing I was already late, and caught the boys in the lift headed to the ground floor.

Hearts shook his head, a small smile playing on his lips. "Aren't you going down?"

The doors closed as he watched me, and I got the impression he knew exactly what I was going to do.

Abandoning the pretense, I caught the next lift down, and managed to get back onto the boat I had hired, unseen. The larger fishing charters were moored by the marina with their own booking office which was fortunately a good few hundred metres up the coast.

I hunkered down until I saw the boys take off in the direction I had headed out in originally and worked my way around the island, heading wide to the north, with the aim of somehow setting myself up to their side for some real protection, not the fluffy position Hearts gave me.

The fuel gauge read halfway, and heedless of the small dose of panic that slid down the back of my throat.

Unwilling to leave them in harm's way, I powered through the tiny white caps that rose in front of me as the ocean breeze whipped around me, and hoped I wasn't too late.

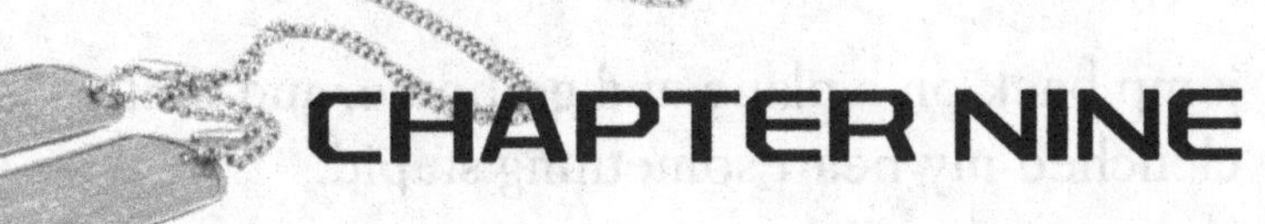

CHAPTER NINE

CHRISSY

I strode through the resort, welcoming the cool air that swept over my skin. Sweat pebbled as my arms broke out in goosebumps. Shaking the shiver away, I hit the elevator button to head up to my room, smiling inanely at the black-suited gentleman who gestured me into the lift.

Getting pissy with Noah wasn't my style. Even in Cambodia, I'd held myself together during my police interrogation better than this, and truth be told, that had been a whole lot worse. Those torturous and terrifying lost hours were something I was keen to never experience again.

If Noah had work to do, then I would only be in his way, and getting in between him and his—investigation? Mission?—would only end in someone getting hurt. It would either be me, or I'd be the cause of one of his friend's injuries, or worse, his. My heart closed up at the thought. No, I was better off away from him, to let him do his job. Afterwards... Was there going to be an *after?* I had no idea if he would jump back on a plane and go home, and that clenched my heart something stupid.

Shaking myself out of my stupor, I started a short list of things I wanted to see and do here from the larger one I had made on the plane before the advent of Noah King. Damnit. Now I was back to ruminating on the sexy soldier. Or spy, or whoever he was.

Every glimpse I had into his life scared me a little more, but it drew me to him as well.

The doors to the lift halted halfway through their closing cycle, a large hand pressed between them. I looked up, the hope that Noah had chased me back to the resort leaping in my chest. More black suits filed into the lift. Disappointment sank through me in a douse of colder air as the lift rose.

I fiddled with my door key, leaning against the back of the lift to give myself room. The cold turned to stuffy with too many bodies in a small space. The doors opened for my floor and I pushed through the suits, relieved to have my space to myself again.

My room was only a few doors down on my left and I opened it with relief. Closing the world out gave me a moment of peace before my brain began to churn. I wasn't here on a romantic getaway; I was here to do my job, blog and get myself to my next destination. Though, at some point, I needed to go home.

I shuddered at the word.

My apartment was darker and lonelier than any sterile resort room. I'd been travelling for so long that the few friends I'd retained had become online only, and though I had plenty of people to chat with, and met a lot of new faces on each trip, I was only part of each life for an instant, moving away before I could make a commitment to anything.

Noah was the person I spent the singular most hours with in over a year.

People and I didn't mix well. That was the crux of why I travelled and blogged, and was lucky enough to make some semblance of a living from it. I didn't do getaways. I ran away. And I'd been running for a long time and saw little reason to stop.

Not even for a pretty face, ripped abs and... I inhaled a sharp breath, and received a lungful of Noah's personal brand of sexy for my efforts.

Damn the man. I needed a show, a massage and six more spectacular hours in his bed. Or mine; I wasn't fazed whose room we used.

Stop, Chrissy. Just...stop.

Hell, I was worse than an underaged kid on Schoolies on the Gold Coast post graduation.

Shaking my head, I stretched. The resort offered yoga, a pool, gym and sauna, but I'd had enough stress for the day. My mind went back to my previous idea, a massage.

I dialled the day spa number on the room phone, and was pleased when they had room immediately. Sending a regretful glance at my laptop, I grabbed my keycard and phone to take pictures with—after all, this was meant to be a work-related excursion—and shoved everything else aside for a few hours.

Including Noah King.

I needed to get my head back on my shoulders.

Some wonderfully relaxed and indeterminable time later, I lay boneless on the massage table, my body flooded with a potent mix of happy hormones. Spa music filled the room with circadian rhythms that were perfect for a reset. My massage therapist was a goddess and the tension had swept from muscles I hadn't known held any until it was gone.

My mind lazily wandered to Noah King, but I could push him away with ease for now. The package included hot rock therapy and a scalp massage, and I'd become pretty much insensible after that.

My therapist patted my oil-covered shoulder. "I'll be back with a cloth to clean you off," she said in her soft, serene voice.

I nodded drowsily, yawning with my head in the cut out at the table, staring down at a little wooden bowl filled with water. Red heilala flowers floated on top. I breathed out and closed my eyes, holding onto my happiness for the next few minutes.

Footsteps entered the room, and then another heavier, distinct pair. I opened my eyes but all I could see was the floating flowers that drifted around this bowl with the force of the footsteps.

That's not my goddess massage therapist.

I pushed up with my hands planted squarely on the edges of the table for leverage. A hand on the back of my head pushed me straight back down.

"What—" I objected, clawing backward at the hand that clutched at the back of my head. My arms windmilled backward, which didn't really work.

A towel was thrown over my body, then another. Finally my clothes were shoved into my hands. "Get up and get dressed," the unknown person said, his deep baritone rumbling over me in a slightly familiar tone. "And hurry, or we leave without the clothes."

I blinked when the hand jabbed the back of my neck in a hard poke. Prickles of cold sweat broke out over me.

"Who the hell are—" I pushed up fully as the hand dropped away, winding the towels around my body in an instant.

Three men dressed in black suits surrounded the massage bed, their combined bulk too much to contain in such a small space. I stared directly down the barrel of a handgun that was probably small but looked like a cannon to me.

"Get dressed. Now," the man holding the gun grated in a harsh voice. I managed to drag my gaze from the black gun to his face, and recognition was instant.

The only other time I saw that face was on the back of a jet ski in the middle of the water, not three hours ago. The cold, dead look in his eyes promised me I wouldn't get a second chance at obeying his commands.

My mind whirling, I yanked my clothes on as best I could beneath the haphazard bundle of towels. When I opened my mouth, the gun waved threateningly. Biting my lip, I nodded, trying to figure out a way to call for help, but my brain jammed, and this time there was no one coming to save me. Noah and his friends were unlikely to turn up a second time.

But they're here because of him.

Right now, I'd take the Cambodian interrogation over this. At least I knew how that one ended.

I stood fully dressed, my body cold and numb with my brain not too far behind. The men surrounded me, closing into my space, and herded me out of the day spa and past the bank of lifts to a single elevator further down the hall. This one smelled like food as I was shoved inside. A trolley full of folded towels stood to one end of the hall.

"Why are you doing this?" I managed to push out between teeth I was surprised weren't chattering. Maybe I'd gone past the point of shock and straight into the realm of the semi-dead as my body expected it to happen at any given point.

Creepy gun man turned to face me, his lips curved in a small, deadly smile, one finger pressed to his lips. He leaned forward to rub the barrel of the pistol down my cheek, his eye tracking the caress with an almost loving glance.

Cold flooded my system, replacing any remaining happy hormones. I wished I'd chased Noah down. I wished I hadn't left him at all. I wished—

A black bag was placed over my head, tied tight around my throat. Propelled forward by too many sets of hands, I stumbled and crashed to the floor, unable to judge where the ground was with no depth perception. My wrists ached and my nose stung as I was hauled upright, and shoved through a doorway that caught me on both shoulders as I twisted in my awkward position. I inhaled enough to try to yell and ended up with a mouthful of cloth for my efforts. My yell died a muffled and pitiful death as I tumbled into the cool edge of a vehicle.

Something slammed into my head a second time, and the black material covering my face was replaced with a void that sucked me down, and down.

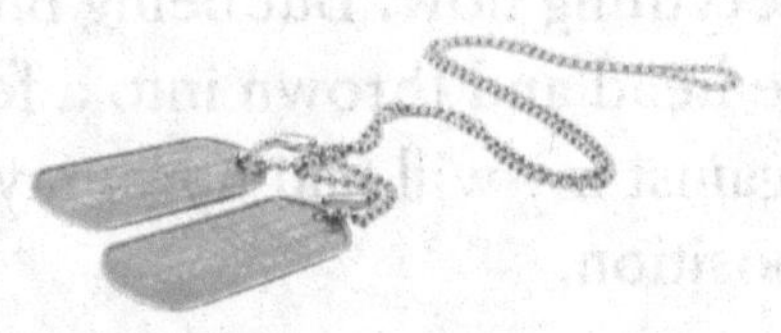

I opened my eyes to a dim room. Light filtered around me, its slanted rays sent spikes of pain that radiated from my nose to the back of my head, and covered everything in between. Pulling my knees beneath me, I tried to push up. The room swayed dangerously around me in a rhythm that set my stomach whirling.

The floor shifted again, the room...cabin shifting with it.

I was on a boat.

I groaned as my forehead found the floor, wave after wave of nausea rolling over me. At least the bag wasn't still on my head in the event that I puked, which was looking likely. Suffocating in my own vomit was not how I was going to go out. Nor was I usually a victim of motion sickness, though I saw its effects many times.

A travel blogger who suffered on a boat or plane wasn't likely to do well, though I was sure there was a market for it, same as there was for everything now. But being hit on the back of the head and thrown into a few vehicles against my will had upset my usually hardy disposition.

There were no brownie points up for grabs as to which boat I was on, either.

A groan tore from my throat as the floor lurched again. I swallowed down my breakfast with King—my God, was this what his life was like all the time? It was too hard to believe that our whirlwind romance had begun less than twenty-four hours ago—and attempted to adult.

Hair fell over my face. I tried to raise my hands to brush it back, only to discover that they were bound in front of me. I studied my fingertips, which had a slight mulberry tint to them, dispassionately. The coarse rope cut deep indents into my wrists, but I could barely feel it. I wiggled fingers cold to the touch when I pressed them to my face, and felt little.

Heavy footsteps that matched the weight of the ones prior to my abduction from the day spa reverberated down a small flight of stairs. The footsteps belonged to the man I expected, except now he was dressed in a pair of tailored, caramel coloured shorts, with a casual white button down shirt over it. His suit heels had been swapped out for boat shoes, similar to the ones King wore earlier in the day. With his dark hair brushed back from his face, and clean shaven, it was difficult to reconcile this man with our jet ski intruder or my assailant of earlier.

I struggled to lift my body into a sitting position. Leaning on my numbed hands, a spike of pain shot along my arm, radiating into a flash of white that obliterated my vision. The boat rocked as the world returned to me, or me to it. My stomach protested, and pain warred with nausea in a sickening battle that existed inside me.

He crouched in front of me, leaning his face down to my level. "Would you like a bucket?" he asked cordially, brushing my hair back from my face as though I suffered from nothing more than a hangover after a frat party.

I wanted to spit in his face, but his dead eyes killed any bravado I had left. A thousand questions tore through my head, but after my hours in Cambodia with the world's best and worst interrogators, I had enough experience to make sure I asked the right questions.

"Why am I here?" I asked. My voice rasped with disuse and I wondered how long I had been out. For the first time, I looked around at where I was, at the few windows that let light filter in from what I assumed was the open deck above.

His gaze never left my face as I studied the room, the hint of a smile played at the corners of his thin lips that didn't match his eyes. He huffed out a breath that could never have been called a laugh.

"You are my lure. I don't like people turning up on my doorstep uninvited. And you and that military brat didn't have an invitation." He stood, leaving me looking at the pristine tops of his white boat shoes.

My mind chugged into action at slug-pace. Was it so obvious that Noah was military or Army or whatever? I supposed that with the close cut hair, clean shaven face and his confident bearing, that to someone who might be looking that it was obvious.

"They won't come." What was I, a cliche movie?

"They?" he drawled.

Shit.

Silence fell between us.

I closed my eyes for a brief moment. There was no taking that one back. I didn't even try.

When I looked back up, he was smiling; a hideous slash in a face it didn't suit.

But this time, it reached his eyes.

"Come on, honey. You're needed up top for display purposes." He caught my wrists, yanking me off the floor with a single tug.

I saw white.

Pain roared in my ears, blocking out everything around me a second time. A twisted gurgling sound reached my ears, my throat rasping again.

When my vision returned, he stared at me, my bound hands clasped between his. He stroked over the purple, numbed flesh, up to my wrist.

"Hurt, does it?" he cooed.

His stare became unnerving, more so than when he held a gun over me. Like he'd trapped a bug, and I was his fascination.

"No," I gritted out, unsure why I was fighting an obvious truth. I wanted to defy this man in some small way, even if it was a token effort.

"Broken, honey?" he murmured, his touch a lover's caress. "How's this?" He twisted my hand a little, slowly rotating my wrist where the ropes bit into my skin.

My knees buckled. I bent to the floor, a high whine ripping from my throat. Unable to control anything, I retched on the floor at his feet.

My aggressor stepped neatly away from my puddle of pain, dragging me up the steps by my wrists.

Sunlight assailed my eyes in glare that ripped a new slice through the ache that had dulled in my head. I whimpered as realization hit me. He used the same endearment that Noah had with me earlier.

How much of a coincidence could that be for a psychopath? Did he know King? Had he been listening?

The thought of this man listening in on our steamy morning session sent my stomach plummeting past my feet. I retched again. Drool dribbled from my lips to dangle from my chin. I swiped it at my shoulder ineffectively.

He still towed me along, taking little notice of my bodily functions.

"Stop." My protest came out as a moan. My knees buckled beneath me as he dragged me across the deck, disregarding my lack of mobility.

My bound hands were lifted above my head and tethered to a railing that surrounded the glassed bridge. The ocean surrounded us, gentle and calm, and utterly isolated. A sob escaped me as he trailed his fingers along my arm in that same intimate caress, twisting and pinching the skin.

Each touch drew whimpers I couldn't control, my pain threshold shattered by the white hot poker speared down the same arm he pinched. I bit my lips, pressing them together, but that seemed to incite him further, the pinches coming cold and brual along my exposed sides.

"Let's hope your friends don't try to sink my boat. Or you'll be the last captain that goes down with it." He tapped my head in mimicry of plopping a hat on it and wandered away, whistling.

The pristine and totally boatless ocean view before me blurred as my vision blurred, salt that wasn't from the ocean assaulting my eyes.

I hovered out of the yacht's line of sight, my pocket buzzing at a ridiculous speed. If I'd been a nineteen fifties housewife sitting on a washing machine, I would have been a happy camper.

Ignoring the boys for the moment—Hearts and Ace would be ready to rip me a new one by now—I started my calculations. The ancient rifle provided a weight heavier than what remained of my conscience at my feet. Making a shot at such a distance while sitting in a glorified dinghy was impossible enough, between both boats moving at irregular rates. I'd be lucky if I didn't end up shooting my own men.

Maybe I could get lucky and ricochet a bullet off a wall, but that took an art into the realm of put-luck, and I refused to gamble with my unit's lives like that. Fortunately, there was no wind to factor in for the moment, though I'd likely have to move within their potential firing range before I started shooting.

But there was zero chance in my mind that the unit wouldn't need support, and I was fucking useless perched on the top of a tower where I couldn't even see a target. Shooting blindfolded in a room full of friendlies would be more effective than that.

My phone buzzed away in my pocket. I groaned, lowering everything to fish it out, scrolling through the long line of messages on an encrypted chat channel Joker had set up for us when he joined the unit. I snorted as I scrolled over their antics, but my smile faded as I hit some of the more serious messages.

Ace: Get back in your tower, Princess. Or I'll change your fucking callsign.

Hearts: Do what the boss says, King. I don't want to penalise you from travel.

Queen: Follow the yellow brick road...

I huffed a laugh. For all his bulllshit, Queen was the boy you wanted most at your back. He was smart as hell, slightly reckless and utterly suicidal. He'd take on an army on his lonesome just to let another soldier walk away unscathed.

Ace: If I have to get on a plane, I'll be pissed.

Joker: Matriarch is listed to a ghost corporation. Fucking nothing.

Knave: I have pictures of your Mister No Name. No name, tho...

Knave: He's not even wanted.

Joker: So disappointing.

Hearts: Ignis Fatuus. Shell corporation headed by...looks like a shit ton of reclusive CEOs, wealthiest world wide, etc., etc. Zero names.

Hearts: What's the difference between a ghost corp and a shell corp?

Joker: NFI.

Ace: He's right. No names. Plenty of footage, plenty of places they turn up with big ass gaps between their appearances. No records, no credit cards, banks, debt...they are damn wisps.

Queen: Follow follow follow follow follow the yellow brick road.

Joker: Rumours the pictures aren't real.

King: Fakes?

I joined the conversation against my better judgement.

Ace: Back in the tower. Now.

Hearts: You'd better be landbound

Joker: Not fakes. These were how they looked, once.

King: The boat is a permanent day spa?

Ace: Move, King. Now.

Joker: Some were doctors, exclusive type worth millions plus. Lots of hermits, who owned a lot of companies. Once. Five years ago, they all went on a little cruise and...

Queen: Poof

Joker: Magic. Stay on the water, man. I got a feeling.

Ace: Ignore him.

Hearts: Ignore him.

I didn't ignore Joker, and I wasn't going back to land. The last time Joker got a fucking feeling, he dragged himself away from an engagemnt sans the rest of his company and missing one leg from the knee down.

Good medical attention meant he didn't have a limp, but he'd lost more than a handful of men and some skin that day.

King: I'm here. It's a shitty shot to take, but I'll make it work. 20 shots is all I've got.

King: Make your suicide run count, fuckers.

Joker: noted.

Hearts and Ace were conspicuously silent.

I grimaced, pocketed my phone, and went back to my calculations. My phone buzzed again and I took Heart's advice, though it hadn't been aimed at me. Well, on the receiving end anyway.

My phone buzzed again in quick succession and fell silent.

It took a whole second before curiosity overwhelmed me.

I yanked it out of my pocket. Joker opened a private channel.

Joker: Danger, Will Robinson. Upstairs boys aren't listening, but I'm used to it.

Joker: We need you. ETA four mins or less. Visual.

Joker: We found a fishing boat and parts of the fishermen. The missing ones. I think.

Joker: It's actually hard to tell.

Rereading the words didn't help the nausea that churned in my stomach. I stared at them a moment longer and sent a message back.

King: I got you, boo. We'll get you a bandaid and some nice cognac.

Joker: Bring the bottle and some matches. I'm pissed we only found this because of your hookup.

My hackles raised at that. Chrissy wasn't just a hook-up. Well, to be fair, that's what it

probably looked like to the boys, but I had full intentions of finding her and making sure we had a third encounter, and a fourth. She'd gotten under my skin that fast, and despite our snark from earlier, I wanted her to stay right where I had her earlier.

Assuming we didn't all end up dismembered in a rowboat in the middle of the Pacific fucking Ocean.

My interim calculations complete, I motored the boat forward at a low pur, aware of how well sound carried over the water. When I had both boats in view, a tight cluster, I started my calculations again. The unit bumped against the *Matriarch*, and I pushed through the fear that I wouldn't get it all done in time. The wind shifted, throwing me out, but when I checked the deck with the binos again, there was no one around. I flicked to the glass housed console, but even the navigation centre was empty.

Movement below drew my attention. I shifted the binos and stared into eyes that, over the past twenty-four hours, I had come to know well.

So well, the terror in her face ripped the remaining breath from my chest.

I fingered the outline of my phone through my pocket, wanting to send off a message to Joker, but I couldn't bear to take my eyes off her, either. What happened if I did and she was gone? What happened if I did and she was...the image Joker tossed so casually into my mind took over. I compressed those images to deal with later, if anything actually happened.

Maybe the boat was deserted. Maybe they left and my unit wouldn't need support after all.

Maybe pink pigs would fly across the sky on pretty striped wings.

How the hell else had Chrissy gotten into the position she was in?

I sharpened the focus on the binos, closing in on her face. My scope might have done the job just as well, but I wasn't game to remove it from its tenuous setting and risk not getting it back on all wobbly. Making the potential shots through iron sights was not on my to-do list.

Chrissy seemed to be just fine—apart from being strung up at the front of the boat. Not quite in the sacrificial figurehead position, but it was bloody well close enough. Her eyes were screwed up against the glare reflecting off the water, but something in her face drew her features tight. It wasn't fear, though I had no doubt the adrenaline that likely flooded her system in a fight-or-flight response was fuelled by that. No this was different, and came from a darker place. Pain.

My chest too tight to draw in a full breath, I studied every inch of her, finally stopping on her hands. Rope lashed around her wrists in tight bonds, her hands above a shade of purple that should only be seen on a vegetable. One hand looked stiff and swollen.

A string of curses fell from my lips.

I let the anger rise, let it out, let it over boil and run out of oomph. When the energy faded, I drew in long, slow breaths, focusing through the rifle scope until my heart rate slowed. My hands were still beneath the unfamiliar weight of a new/old weapon that was a comfort in my hands.

My boys flicked in and out of the shadows across the deck. A quick glance confirmed that Knave was left on the boat. Dying sunlight glinted off more than one blade as the unit spread out around the boat, the flashes more red than bright white in the late afternoon.

I should have sent Joker that message, but it was too late now, and with luck, they could come up on her with no clashes with our newfound enemy, who appeared to know a hell of a lot more about us than we did about him.

Unless, somehow, Chrissy was involved.

The old doubts, the betrayal I pushed down less than a dozen hours before, resurfaced. I drew the scope back to study her. Stretched out on her toes in what had to be a horrendously painful position, her feet looked cramped. I fiddled with the scope, focusing on the trail of tears that traced over her cheekbones, and my heart clenched again.

The man we met earlier appeared as a shadow behind her, twisting her hair to pull her head back. Her mouth opened in protest or shock—I couldn't hear from my distance—as he laughed at her response and spat in her face.

Her eyes closed, but when she opened them again, her gaze was full of hatred that just covered her desperation and she returned the favour to him.

I watched, sickened as he smiled slowly, then reached up to tweak her swollen hand.

Chrissy's knees drew up to her chest, her mouth open in a silent scream that echoed in my head despite the distance between us.

How the hell I doubted her, I had no idea.

My heart filled with rage again and I forced it back with little success. Breathing hard through my nose, I attempted to pull my shit together. A red flash caught my attention.

I swung my sights away from my girl, swearing as I found my three boys locked in hand to hand combat while I'd focused on the wrong thing.

Or maybe it was the right thing.

On cue, my breath slowed, my training kicking in. My vision cleared as I looked through the scope, waiting for a wider than usual gap in the fight to take the shot.

Then the gap came, and I fired.

My first shot was too wide for where I aimed and tore splinters off the cabin wall above Hearts' head. He froze for a second, flipped the bird to the ocean, and reengaged his target.

I dropped everything and moved the boat forward as far as I dared to remain effective. Before I grabbed the rifle, bullets sprayed the ocean around me, pinging off the hull of my small boat. I ignored it all and got back into position.

Without any further assistance from me, Hearts' sparring partner went down, and he stepped over the body in search of another. He headed toward Chrissy again, and I left him to do his job, and hoped he would do it a hell of a lot better than I did mine.

Swearing wouldn't help me or my team. I swung to the next target where Joker fought in a frenzy that had always been his style, sinking deeper into my pose, letting the weight of the rifle settle in my hands.

When the breath left my lungs in a hollow whisper, I took the shot.

Joker's opponent dropped.

More bullets sprayed around me, and I was thankful that, at a few hundred metres, the shooters weren't accurate. A bullet sang past my ear and I held still, returning my attention to the deck. Protect first, then worry about my shooters.

I received a similar salute from Joker as he moved on and I focused on Queen. He danced around his opponent. It was a quick step that got in the way of every clean shot I had a chance at pulling off.

The man's blade swiped at Queen's stomach. He leaped back, his Hawaiian shirt hanging in tatters. The tip of the blade caught his arm. I saw the moment he leapt back, caught his heel on the deck, and stumbled.

His fighter leered at him for a second he shouldn't have taken. He dropped to the deck with his friend as mine rose back to his feet and waved.

"Nice to be appreciated," I murmured to no one at all as I shifted back to find Chrissy. More bodies were piled around Joker's and Hearts' feet. Chrissy's assailant was nowhere in sight.

Two men stood on the roof of the boat, black submachine guns in their hands. My turn. I dropped them in rapid succession, though it took me four additional shots I didn't want to waste. My presence was unlikely to be a secret, but my position might still be, and I wanted to keep it that way for as long as possible.

A white wake formed around the back of the pleasure cruiser. I watched, gripping the stock of my rifle too tight as the man who assaulted Chrissy disappeared out of my line of sight in a smaller speed boat.

The drone of a low flying aircraft drew me away from my sights. I raised my head, watching a small chopper, out of my range, hover well past the *Matriarch*, and I assumed he would escape.

The string of curses erupted from my lips again.

My pocket buzzed. I picked it up without bothering to look at the screen.

"He's gone." Joker's voice crackled in my ear, his accent thickening.

"We were hopelessly outgunned and under prepared. This should have been a walk in the fucking park."

"I know," he murmured. "We got your girl."

"Thanks." I stopped. "Wait, next time?"

"Well, we aren't giving up this easily, are we?" he asked lightly, though something tightened in his tone.

"Tell me," I demanded.

"He left you a note."

"Me? What the hell?"

"Yeah, you two are bosom buddies. King and Grimeau. Sounds like a Musketeers fantasy."

"He left me a note?" I repeated, turning his name over in my head.

Grimeau.

"Yes. Catch up. Actually, come up here. Queen's taking care of Chrissy. Hearts is doctoring Knave."

"What happened to him?"

"While you were dozing, he got himself knocked out," Joker snapped.

Fuck.

I didn't bother waiting for an apology. "I'll be right there."

Joker hung up before I could. I started the boat's engine, wary of the thin stream of smoke that drifted from one side, and prayed I wouldn't run out of fuel before I reached Chrissy.

CHAPTER ELEVEN

CHRISSY

I sat on a small, upturned crate while Joker held my wrist in a gentle grip. Ice water ran along my arm, but I could barely feel it. Hearts jumped from studying my hand with a pained expression, and helping his friend. He kept talking to me, but I couldn't help my attention from wandering over the darkened waters.

The sun had set shortly after Noah's team had infiltrated the boat, and released me from where I hung. Though it probably hadn't been that long, my shoulders screamed when I was released. My toes had gone numb early on, and the rush of circulation redirected pain from my hand and shoulders to my legs for a brief respite before the cycle started all over again.

Queen had cleaned me up. His touch was gentle as he alternated between telling me a very dark version of the *Princess and the Pea* fairytale, and singing partial phrases from *The Rocky Horror Picture Show* in between.

"I really need to get you back to the island," Hearts murmured, still fussing over my hand. He found a small light that illuminated an area of the deck enough to see what he was doing.

"I'll be fine," I said in a stage whisper that wobbled horribly. I forced a grin over the lot as I scanned the water, but there was no sight nor sound of a boat or anything else nearby.

Joker ruffled my hair. "You'll keep." He took up sentry duty by the rail, staring over it, and I was glad of the company.

"She'd better," a faint voice barely made it to my ears. I peered forward, but couldn't see a thing. "Down here. Help me up, fucker." Noah's voice grew stronger, a banging at the hull announcing his arrival.

"What the hell are you doing down there?" Joker asked, leaning over the rail like he was talking to a mate at a bar, and made no move to help.

"Ran out of fucking fuel. Motor got shot up. So did the boat." Noah sounded absolutely disgusted with himself as he made a shopping list of his calamities.

Joker nodded, patting Noah's shoulder in sympathy.

A giggle escaped me at the absurdity of them both.

A cold glass pressed into my palm, and I closed my hand around the object in reflex. Queen guided my hand to my lips, always gentle, and I sipped the champagne with some relief.

"That's my girl. Drink up. It's medicinal," he murmured, this last aimed at Hearts, who returned to staring at me with his pained look.

Joker looked over his shoulder atr me and rolled his eyes. "Come on. Before you turn into shark bait."

"You think I wanna look like you?" Noah hauled himself over the railing with Joker's help and tumbled to his knees in a wet heap.

He pushed up from where he sat, nothing more than a sodden mess that trudged forward to collapse at my feet. His head fell against my thighs, nestled there, sparing me a glance before he closed his eyes, and breathed out.

Noah's arms never left me the entire trip back to Australia. We hopped from island to island in an assortment of emergency helicopters to military aircraft, and he was by my side, touching me for every second.

The car trip across Brisbane to the nearest hospital for x-rays and assorted medical attention let him press me to his side without injuring me. A cast and another car trip in the small hours, we were on a boat trip to Fraser Island, which was apparently the boys' training centre. They refused to leave either of us, and tagged along the entire time.

"I'm not letting you go, you know that?" Noah's sapphire blue eyes pierced me, refusing to release me as I let him hold me to his side.

Watching the tall, stubborn soldier pass out at my feet had been both one of the most terrifying and happy experiences of my life. Knowing he came back for me, that he came straight to me once he was on the boat, had rearranged a few of my priorities.

"I'm good," I murmured. "Keep holding on, soldier."

His arm tightened around my waist, he pressed his lips to my hair, and stilled.

It took me a moment to realise he had fallen asleep. I closed my eyes, sinking into his chest as pain, a hefty dose of painkillers that didn't take quite the edge off, shock and pure exhaustion washed over me.

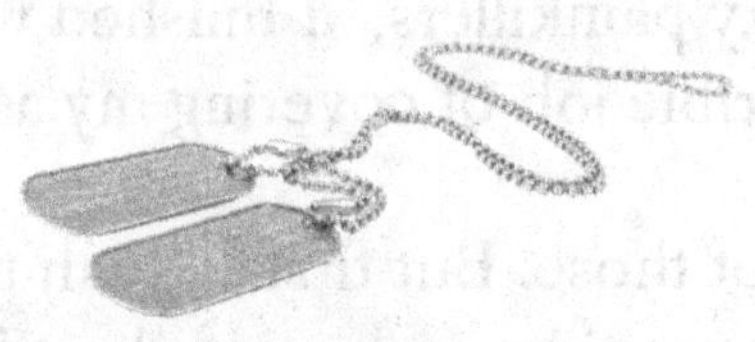

I woke warm, cuddly, and wrapped in a band of muscles with an urgent need to pee. Wriggling slightly in Noah's grip, I managed to free myself. Clambering over him in the double bed that was pushed against the wall wasn't so easy. He'd taken the lion's share in sleeping diagonally across the mattress, but to be fair, it was probably the only way he actually fit in the thing without his legs and feet hanging off the end.

It didn't solve the problem of getting over his sleeping form, however.

I wriggled over him in an arch, completely forgot about my broken wrist, and tumbled to the floor with a cry, tears springing to my eyes.

It came as a surprise there were any left at all.

"Chrissy, honey," Noah murmured, gathering me in his arms.

I stiffened at the endearment, having heard it last on another man's lips. "I need more of those snazzy painkillers," I finished weakly, doing a terrible job of covering my ass.

"I've got those. But first," Noah traced his hand along my side, and my body stiffened at his touch. "What's this? I understand if you don't want me to touch you, Chrissy. Not after you've seen what I can do."

I *had* seen what he could do, bad guys falling like flies with each second as he removed obstacles from his team. The man—Grimeau—got away, but not before managing to leave his mark on each of us in a disturbingly personal way.

"It's not that. But he—" I hesitated, unwilling to use the man's name, but Noah nodded, seeming to understand, "He called me that. After you had, where I..." *Where I cherished it.* But I couldn't bring myself to say that out loud. I swallowed. "...and it all got mixed up in my head. That's all. I promise," I added when he didn't look convinced.

"I get it, Chrissy. Seriously." Noah ran a hand over his head, looking away from me.

He grabbed my painkillers and water bottle and helped me to swallow them. Everything felt thick and ungainly.

"No, you don't. He assaulted me. Stole me. You saved me. Everyone, really. Is it hard to be so removed and to not be there with everyone if someone gets hurt?" I asked, remembering the question I wanted to ask him the night before, but everything had gotten so muddled.

Noah leaned forward to kiss my forehead. "It can be hard, especially if I'm the one who screwed up. But I can see more from there than they can. The bird's eye view of what's going on. Often I have a spotter, someone with radio comms beside me, and we can help. Other times, it's just me. Joker helps me on occasion."

"Is that why you're so close?" I asked, leaning up to press a kiss to his lips.

A kiss that quickly developed into something deeper, and Noah drew back with a harsh laugh. "Damn, girl." He kissed me again, and again, until I was glad I was sitting on him. He curled around me, pushing me back but I waved my cast at him.

"Toilet stop first. Please?"

"Down there, to the right. I'll make you some breakfast. Then..." His gaze roamed over me as I managed to get off the bed, the sinful promise in his gaze hastening my departure from the room, my heart pounding.

My trip to the bathroom was brief. I paced back through the house, careful of my footsteps, unsure of the time or how much everyone needed to sleep in. Every room I passed was empty.

As I neared the kitchen, conversation reached me, and I smiled.

I could hear Noah and Joker's banter a room away. The Tran twins, Knave and Queen, added to the chorus. The only voice missing was Hearts, who seemed to be a greatly silent man, and Ace.

Ace, who had been at the door when we walked in the night before, was a giant of a sentinel who admitted me over his threshold. That alone was enough to intimidate me, but when I stared at the older officer, I recognised the layers of pain and experience of a war-hardened soldier, one who suffered more than the rest of his unit combined.

I knew, because I saw that same look in veterans around the world. Veterans who returned home to make a shell of a life for themselves, to push their way back into society without really being part of it. Because they felt they had to. Because they felt they should, but couldn't.

I'd had too many drinks with the men and women who ran small tourist operations around the world to recognise one infallible truth. No matter where they fought, or who they fought for, a soldier was the same as any other, their life defined by their experiences, and the guilt that trailed after them.

Ace's burden of guilt was greater than any soldier I'd ever met.

And he was Noah King's boss.

So I'd taken the coward's way out, and huddled beneath the bulk of the man I was starting to know and had already fallen for and was in utter awe of.

When Noah had fallen asleep, and I hadn't been able to, I'd clambered gracelessly around his sleeping form to escape the facility that housed the bedrooms and living areas. Fresh, salty air clung to my skin in a sticky coat, the humidity of the night air still and close.

And I loved it.

Ace arrived beside me at some indeterminate point during my blank musings. And when I hadn't been able to talk, he had, filling the hours until my eyelids grew heavy, and I excused myself.

Then, he asked his question.

I slipped into the kitchen, taking the mug of coffee Queen held out to me without looking, and took the spare seat between Hearts and Noah. I was comfortable around the big man, who I would never have thought could have moved as fast as he had on the boat.

Noah's arm curled around my shoulder.

A plate of food arrived in front of me and I stared at the mountain Knave presented to me.

"This can't be all for me," I protested.

"Only you, darling." Queen placed two white pills in my hand. "Down the hatch and ask the boys for help if you need it. They're bored now that the action is over and done."

"And you're not?" I asked, and cringed. Hell, I hadn't been in the room for a full minute and already I was insulting people. "I'm sorry, that was—"

"Totally justified, my dear. Eat." Queen pointed his spatula and fixed me with a hard stare.

Aware of too many pairs of eyes on me, I started to eat. Within moments, I was enjoying it. "This is incredible. Thank you," I smiled, raising my coffee mug in a salute.

King and Joker took the opportunity to remove the bacon from my plate. Joker dove back for a second run at my garlic buttered mushrooms, and I jabbed the back of his hand with my fork. "Uh uh." I shook my head. "No one gets my mushrooms."

Noah laughed, tugging me closer. "But I can steal your bacon?"

"It's a privilege." I poked the back of his hand gently to my point. "Don't push it, Princess."

The table broke up in a roar.

King leaned back, taking it all with a slightly goofy look on his face. He ran his hand over his head, his cheeks pink.

Across the table, Hearts rose, his face closed. His gaze caught mine and for a long moment, I wondered if he was privy to the conversation I had with Ace in the hours before dawn, though conversation was pushing it. He'd talked, and I'd listened.

Noah tugged me against his shoulder. "I need to go for a run."

I titled my head back to look up at him. "You swam, what, two kilometers yesterday, and today you need to run?"

"It's a habit." He shrugged. "Besides, it was more like three. There was a rip or current, something that kept dragging the boat backward while I pussy footed about trying to fix it."

"Whinge, whinge, whinge." Joker snagged a mushroom while I was distracted.

I waved my fork, but it was a fairly pathetic threat.

Hearts reappeared in the kitchen doorway and gestured to Noah. "He wants to see you. Now." Hearts' face held no emotion whatsoever.

The little clone of Ace. What a momentous moment.

Joker grimaced, giving me an ass tap as Noah passed him.

I refrained from punching him in the face. The boy's roughhousing was wearing off on me in a really bad way. I bit my lip, tugging it into my mouth.

"I'll write you a pretty eulogy," Queen called.

"Appreciate it," King called. He wound an arm around my waist, his mouth claiming mine in a show of possession and defiance.

I went with it. After all he had done, surely he deserved more than a roasting...or worse. Despite everything, I doubted anyone could extract the military aspect from Noah if they tried.

"Oh, you too, sweetheart," Ace called from the office.

Noah froze, turned to stone in my arms. "What the hell is he doing?" he grated out into my ear.

A shiver ripped down my spine as he held me tighter. "I'm sure it's fine," I said nervously, clinging to his shirt like a damned damsel in distress, but that moment had long passed. This one was of my own doing. I breathed in a long, slow breath, and gestured forward. "Shall we meet the devil?"

Noah flashed me a quick grin, and tugged me forward, his hand wrapped firmly around mine.

EPILOGUE

KING

I stepped into Ace's office and was immediately assaulted by a tongue in my face.

"Helix. Down!" Ace called, in the sort of voice you might call off an armoured guard, or a terrorist attack.

"Haven't lost it, sir." I grinned, stroking the Belgian Malinois' velvety muzzle.

She nuzzled into my palm, sniffed at Chrissy and moved on, circuiting the room to curl up at Ace's feet again.

"Don't smarmy up to him," a bored voice at my back drew my spine straighter. "That level of bullshit doesn't suit you."

I knew that voice well, because I'd spent the better part of a month working a mission—case, *whatever*—with the ex-special ops turned task force head when he had fought against his own demons. A smile curved my lips. I fought it back for good measure, squeezing Chrissy's fingers between mine.

"Got bored with married life already, McNamara?" I asked, not turning around to look at him.

What I'd seen Liam McNamaara manage to achieve with a unit of Aussie cops less than six months before had been nothing shy of magnificent. Z Unit completed missions no one should be asked to do, but we worked our assses off anyway. We crossed a whole lot of grey lines, and we did it with the country's blessing, whether they knew they gave it or not.

Liam's boys backed him over one hundred percent when he walked off the job, and had been prepared to give up their careers and their lives for him. I'd scoffed my way through the job, but the truth was, their sacrifice stalled me. My smile faded. Would we be the same? How would any one of us react to pushing the envelope past a reasonable point?

Liam McNamara had been a soldier, an officer, a cop. A task force head. And despite wearing his own personal tragedies, he chose to lead a second time. The men who worked with him saw him less as a boss and more as a brother.

I stared at Ace across his desk, and he returned my unflinching gaze.

Would we do that for him if he went off the reservation? I damn well hoped so, and looking back over the last week, I suspected we would. I wanted us to have that sense of unfailing camaraderie that Liam's unit had. They didn't flaunt it; but then, they hadn't needed to. It was evident in every gesture, every conversation. A pat on the shoulder between men who were more than friends, who considered each other family.

We needed that, if we were going up against a man like Grimeau and whoever the hell he represented.

I doubted he was more than a frontline floozy, albeit a dangerous one.

The power of a few words on the paper slipped between Chrissy's tired hands had a powerful impact on each of us.

34 Ciputat. Bengran.

The asshole had been sweet enough to address his little love note to me and sign his name at the bottom.

Grimeau.

I clenched my teeth to ward off the memory. Ciputat was a small locality in Indonesia. We had dropped a building we assumed was empty, and hadn't checked, at the recommendation of a man called Bengran, in an effort to close off a drug ring in the wake of a large exchange of cash.

There hadn't been a single drop of evidence when we walked back through the rubble, nor any cash.

All we found were the remains of locals who weren't supposed to be there in the first place, and Bengran. We weren't meant to be in the country at the time, and we'd had a hell of a lot of trouble getting back out before we caused an international incident. Some poor politician would have done a poor job of explaining while we rotted in a dark cell somewhere, at best.

And now our new friend knew the details of the death of our old friend, and we were getting all cozy.

Cozy, with a side serving of cyanide.

Which brought me back to being ripped a new one by Ace in his office. Still, the thought lingered. If we were going up against Ignis Fatuus, we had to be as strong as Liam's team, and we'd only be stronger undivided.

That was if I didn't get my ass handed to me and was walked off the property within the next few minutes.

I wondered if Liam would give me a job.

"Thought I'd come to check on the kindergarteners." Behind me, Liam yawned, his back popping audibly as he stretched.

Ace looked like he'd been slapped.

"Listen, you pompous, overdressed ass—" Ace planted clenched fists on his desk, either side of his planner, pushing himself up by his knuckles. His face reddened, he breathed hard through his nose, and his presence was nothing to be baulked at. The bull's final rein on his control right before the red shirt was waved teasingly in front of him.

"Your boy saved my life. Did a damn fine job," Liam murmured.

Ace huffed air through his nose, and stayed silent.

Chrissy giggled behind me, a slap announcing her belatedly covering her mouth.

Ace closed his and sat back down.

Liam smirked. I could almost hear it.

"He's a good boy." Ace fixed Liam with an assessing stare that made many a staff sergeant run for cover.

Liam didn't flinch.

"He is," Liam agreed, drawing his phone from his pocket, and tapping at it with the speed of a small cyclone. He didn't look up. "I think you have something to say to Noah and Chrissy?"

Ace resembled a guppie.

I couldn't have kept the grin off my face if I wanted to.

Chrissy pressed to my back, clinging to my arm as her body shook in tiny tremors.

"I don't usually let my staff giggle at me in my office, Miss Pilgrim."

I opened my mouth to argue with him and froze.

Behind me, Liam tapped away far too noisily for my taste. I reigned in my irritation and addressed Ace instead, trying to remain calm.

"Your staff?"

"Hasn't she told you?" Ace's smile resembled Liam's smirk. I bit my tongue to halt the rise of my irritation further. "Miss Pilgrim has agreed to help us organise our travel a little more...effectively. She'll set up your activities to both better suit your cover and to provide you a reason for being in a place, as well as several exit strategies. Your holidays will look like real ones. From now on, you fly commercial. Our very own ghost corporation, to combat Ignis Fatuus. Joker and Mister

McNamara will be instrumental in helping her set up."

"I have the room next to yours in Cairns," Chrissy murmured, squeezing my arm. I recognised the moment her tremors of laughter gave way to nerves. Desperate to take her in my arms and reassure her, I held myself rigid before Ace and Liam. Something about inbred training from my army brat life came into play. It tore at my heart that Liam spoke to my father last, rather than me. But that was a choice I made a long time ago. Looking at it from the other side of the fence wasn't so easy. I gripped Chrissy's hand tighter.

"We don't have a lot of space here, Major. Where would you like her to sleep?"

Liam clapped me on the back of the head on his way out.

Ace grinned.

Light fingers stroked the short hair that covered my stinging scalp. "Ow?" Chrissy murmured.

"Ow," I said ruefully, glancing over at her.

It was a mistake.

The moment I broke eye contact with Ace was the moment he jumped back in.

"I won't have any screwing around in my unit, ma'am!" he roared.

I took the slur for what it was, and towed Chrissy out the door before my boss lost his shit entirely. Once she was out of his line of sight, I sent a kiss over my shoulder to Ace, a la Queen.

His face reddened further, though I knew I'd pay for it later on.

Liam stood on the sandy path outside the training camp in his charcoal suit and white button-down shirt. His black work shoes were impeccable. It was the front I suspected he presented to the rest of the world on a daily basis.

And I suspected the special ops sniper who was desperate to save his men and his family face was one he showed to a select few.

I was privileged to see that side of him.

"Did you come up here to save my ass or to give my boss sass?" I asked softly, already knowing the answer.

Lima turned back with a smirk. "I'm sure you'll repay the favour someday."

I studied him, the steel grey eyes, the scars worn with pride he might have finally accepted hid beneath his skin, and wondered what Grimeau would think of this man, if he'd register him as dangerous.

I sure as hell did, and I'd seen him at his weakest moments.

"And here I thought we were even." The regular bravado rose to the surface as it always had with him. He pissed me off less than my father had, and more than the boys I worked shoulder to shoulder with, more like a big brother popping in to check on me.

I was okay with that.

A glint from his wedding ring, still reasonably fresh and polished, reminded me that Liam McNamara was in fact human, despite his unemotional show to the counter.

He was still a fucker I never wanted to cross paths with on any night, dark or otherwise.

"Keep telling yourself that, Junior." Liam nodded, the corners of his mouth still curled as he turned and walked away from the training yard.

I'm sure you'll return the favour one day.

I was sure I would too, but until then, our relationship was...complicated.

"It'll be fun," I called after him.

A small hand linked through mine. I drew Chrissy into me, settling her back against my chest. The curve of her ass was only antagonising until I could take her to bed later, but until then...I tucked her closer into me, revelling in her soft curves, her body arching against mine in a subconscious reflex. I hoped. Because if this girl was playing me, then I was a whole section of the orchestra she could have her way with. "Are you staying?"

I searched her dark eyes, suddenly unsure. How many times was the rug going to be pulled out from under me today? I needed a magic carpet.

Chrissy lifted onto her toes, her hips swaying suggestively. I caught them between my hands and squeezed hard. "I'm staying."

"In my room?"

"The one next door. You heard Ace."

"And I'll ignore him."

"Is this going to be my new habit?"

"Why do you think you got the room next to mine? It has an adjoining door."

"Oh," Chrissy sighed. "Well, in that case..." She tilted her head back, her lips parted and I took the invitation until she sighed softly in my arms.

"Good girl." I nuzzled her neck.

For the first time in a long time, I was able to accept my own small slice of happiness that came bundled with sparkling eyes, a mind to rival Liam's, and a dazzling smile. I leaned down and kissed her, and the usual fear that the future would be torn away from me wasn't there for the first time since I lost Dad.

Chrissy smiled up at me, nestled against my chest. A long shiver rippled over her. I wasn't sure whether it was from my kisses or my words. I was more than happy to test them both out later on.

I hope you loved Noah and Chrissy's story. Please do head over to <u>Amazon to leave a review</u>. They feed authors, and a few words of what you guys loved makes my day!

Read <u>JOKER</u> for more Z-boy action and meet the man who never stops smiling...

ACKNOWLEDGEMENTS

Thank you for reading what was meant to be the first book in Z Boys! (Hint: A Table for Ten is FREE on Amazon! Go grab it now if you haven't downloaded it already). Coming off the back of King's slip into the Blue Blooded Brothers world as Liam's temporary partner, it made sense that he desperately needed his own series. And because some of you loved their banter so much that you messaged me to ask, (read beg here, and keep those coming, i adore those messages the most!) I had to return the favour and slip Liam into the Z Boys books too. Hint: he's becoming a regular now!).

As always, no book is complete without a team of amazing people behind it. Kay, thank you for persisting with the images to get this one right, and for jinning around with me. It's made all the difference and I love love love it!

Crit Chicks, beta team, and Sirens- y'all are my besties. I adore you and can't put a book out without your eyes on the words!

Lily - thank you for editing in the midst of trials no daughter should ever have to go through. Serious gratitude!

Jo - you've been a critical part of my team for two full years and to bring you on board has been a joy! Thank you for proofing every word for me when my own eyes were too blurry to pick out the mistakes.

Hubs and family. All of you. We moved house in the midst of writing this book, and settled during edits. Plus Covid, living in a construction zone and of course, all the homemade inspo I can ever need. *Thank you.* I love you all so much!

Sofia xx

ABOUT THE AUTHOR

USA Today Bestselling author Sofia Aves writes fast-paced police romances, sizzling military units, steamy cowboys with a Montana backdrop and the occasional cheeky god. She loves reading Indie authors and hides her collection of college romance books beneath an ever-growing TBR pile. Sofia is the marketing manager for Romance Writers of Australia and has a regular author marketing column in their monthly magazine. She writes kidlit for charity and has over eighty publications across three not-so-super-secret pen names.

Sofia is a mum of three crazies in a returned veteran household, and has an overly large fur baby who thinks she's a teacup puppy. After eighteen years of planning and dreaming, Sofia and her husband will put the finishing touches on their very own alpaca park this year. Sofia lives near Brisbane, Australia.

Sign up to Sofia's newsletter and get a FREE Blue Blooded Brothers book.

Haven't read the Z Boy's prequel? Get it for free here:

A TABLE FOR TEN

<u>www.sofiaves.com</u>

Follow Sofia on

<u>BookBub</u>

<u>Twitter</u>

<u>Instagram</u>

Read Sofia's Series

Blue Blooded Brothers

Red Hart Ranch

Texan Devils

Christmas Romance

Shortbread Shakedown

Secret Santa

Paranormal Romance

Trickster's Law

A Portrait in Ash & Lace

Blue Blooded Brothers

COLLISION

book 1

POLITICS & PAPERWORK

Novella

BLINDSIDED

book 2

SENTINEL

book 3

IMPACT
book 4
RECKONING
book 5